NOTES FROM A MODERN CHIMURENGA:

Collected Struggle Stories

Tendai Rinos Mwanaka

Cover art by Tendai Mwanaka

Mwanaka Media and Publishing Pvt Ltd,
Chitungwiza Zimbabwe

*

Creativity, Wisdom and Beauty

Publisher: Tendai R Mwanaka

Mwanaka Media and Publishing Pvt Ltd *(Mmap)*

24 Svosve Road, Zengeza 1

Chitungwiza Zimbabwe

mwanaka@yahoo.com

www.africanbookscollective.com/publishers/mwanaka-media-and-publishing

https://facebook.com/MwanakaMediaAndPublishing/

Distributed in and outside N. America by African Books Collective

orders@africanbookscollective.com

www.africanbookscollective.com

ISBN: 978-1-77906-482-0

EAN: 9781779064820

DISCLAIMER

All views expressed in this publication are those of the author and do not necessarily reflect the views of *Mmap*.

Table of Contents

Introduction

This is an extensive collection of Zimbabwe's political struggle short stories and covers the modern Chimurenga period from the formation of tribal trust lands (The Tortoise), the liberation wars (Zanzibar, Eating Whilst Running), the Gukurahundi massacre (Gukurahundi), the late 1990s democratic struggles pitting ZANUPF against the MDC (The List, Mbuya Chitungwiza, Operation Murambatsvina, Notes from Mai Mujuru's Breast, Breaking the Silence), the individual struggle within this democratic struggle (Mushazhike, Nyadzonya), the resultant migration and exilitic stories (Limpopo Bones, Germinston 1401), the corruption (Nyakasikana, Tree of the Year), the mismanagement of the country, the beatings and killings (Leonard, Karidza, Raising A Cain again), and the continuing democratic struggles

The stories are visceral, dramatic, unflinching and indict, are mostly written in spare language. These were stories that were and are real, as a people decides to move from one all-encompassing deeply entrenched system to another, and records the life that this people goes through on their journey. There is no space for me to embellish or create ideological trophies other than those that cuts back to the real life. The struggles, like many of my stories and other writings are written from the perspective of the common man in the street, the subalterns- not from the elites' perspective, and this makes the stories relatable and the struggle be owned by the everyman.

The collection is built from previously published stories, the biggest chunk comes from the first collection of short stories *Keys In The River: Notes From A Modern Chimurenga*, (Savant Books USA, 2012): *The List; The Tortoise; Zanzibar; Eating Whilst Running; Gukurahundi; Mushazhike; Breaking The Silence; Nyadzonya; Mr. Zimyama; Mbuya Chitungwiza; A Look In The Mirror; The Dark Haired Girls; Limpopo's Bones; Germinston 1401*. Thus therefore the title is borrowed from Keys in the River's subtitle, *Notes From A Modern Chimurenga*. Chimurenga is Shona word for struggle as I noted in the original *Keys in the River* introduction in 2012. Another sizable chunk comes from my second collection, *Finding A Way Home* (Langaa RPCIG, Cameroon 2015): *Chitungwiza; Operation Murambatsvina; Notes from Mai Mujuru's breast; A Hero Of Zeroes; Nyakasikana; Hell's Heaven-Sent Refugees; Tree of the Year*. And a few more comes from my third collection of short stories, *A Conversation…, A Contact* (Mwanaka Media and Publishing, Zimbabwe, 2018): *Raising A Cain Again; Leonard; Karidza*. The stories were written over a period of nearly 25 years, from 1994-2018 and thus have shifting views and opinions fed from what was happening through this journey

We are still trundling along a vectored horizon, so the stories will continue being written but this is an opportunity to look back at where we came from, take a breather, rearrange and realign our struggle to fit to where we are and where we want to go. The stories will always be told.

Chapter 1: THE LIST

We don't do torture, we do enhanced interrogation, Madam." He was back again early in the morning of the second day of my abduction. Last night, he came to see me after ignoring me for the whole of that day, leaving me locked in my cell without food, without water, without anything to get by, with only my fingernails for food.

They forcefully had come to our offices, yesterday morning at our workplace Budiriro Trust in Harare central and forcefully abducted us. They took everyone who worked at that organization who was in the offices that morning, accusing us of working in connivance with western governments. They said that we were leaking information on human rights abuses, that we had developed a list of the abused and the abusers. But our work was to help those who had undergone human rights abuses to deal with their traumatic experiences, not feed western governments with details which they were accusing us of.

Last night, late at night, he had visited my cell. I was given a separate cell from everyone else. Since I was the director of this organization, maybe they didn't want me to be with my subordinates because they were afraid I would influence them to refuse to divulge information about the whereabouts of this list of victims of human rights abuses which they had accused us of compiling.

"So, where is the list?"

"I don't know of any list."

I didn't know of any list. I knew they had scoured all our offices, all our hard manuals and mail, all our computers looking for that list. I was sure they hadn't found any list even with my subordinates because no such list existed. So, they had now come to me, to search for the list on me.

"We know you have been compiling a list of human rights abuses, compiling the names of the abusers which you have been sending to your western friends."

"We are not doing anything of that sort. We are not compiling any lists. All that we do is to help the victims, only that! I don't know about the list that you are talking of."

"You think you are cleaver, do you? You had better think fast, woman, because tomorrow morning when I return here, it will be either the list or war. If I were you, I would conclude this issue as soon as possible so that you won't have to face our wrath. We don't do torture, we do enhanced interrogation..."

He left me last night with the threat hanging in the air. Now, he was back and tailing him was his pig of an assistant. He looked fearsome today and his assistant was smiling and smirking. He was looking at me lustfully. It made me shiver. The thought of that pig touching me convulsed through to the pit of my stomach.

"Have you decided about the list?"

"I told you yesterday that there is no list!"

"So, you still don't want to talk? I warned you yesterday about that. Hulk here will bleed the list from you if he has to. I am not going to waste my time. From here on, I will leave you with Hulk."

Just as abruptly as he came, he left, leaving me with the beast. Hulk was his assistant, the interrogator it seemed. During that split moment, I tried to think of what kind of punishment now awaited me.

I didn't know what to do, but to face him with the truth. Hulk came closer to where I was sleeping on top of the bare floors, legs chained to an embedded pole as if I was a fugitive. He had this insane light in his eyes. Then, he started touching me without any preamble. He touched my breasts, my butt, and thighs. This monster kissed me forcefully.

I fought him and he liked the fighting. It teased him all the more so he wore me down slowly and that continued for over an hour. Then, as I had nothing left in me to fight with, he mounted me, raping me.

For a long time, he was inside me painfully thrusting until he released. He rested for a little while, but continued teasing me slowly and insulting me verbally. I felt so dirty, so unworthy of respect, so like shit, like a slut. He continued touching me even when I remained still, silent, afraid of inciting him by fighting him again. I felt like vomiting, but I forced it back because that might have aroused him.

He heated up again and entered me again and again until when he was spent. When he had finished doing his thing, he left me and told me that, upon his return, he needed the list or else all hell would break loose. I wondered what was worse than what he had already done to me.

He returned back in the early afternoons. He returned with a little food for me, just a couple of swallows of Sadza and boiled cabbages, salted with no oil. I gulped everything greedily and, in a minute or two, had finished it. I was so hungry; I hadn't eaten anything for a day and a half. I asked for water, but he laughed that off scornfully.

"Rather you should be giving me the list, not demanding for water."

"I don't have the list. Please! Won't you understand that and let us out for we don't have the list you are looking for."

He laughed that off too and said. "Maybe you enjoyed making love to me this morning."

He said that as he started touching me again. His hands moved over my body with a knack for lust. I was so scared of having to go through that sick thing with him again so I lied to him.

"I am HIV positive!"

But, he bowled over with laughter.

"What's funny?" I asked him, bewildered with him.

"Well, let me guess...you sort of thought if you said you had AIDS it would scare me, did you?"

I couldn't confirm that.

"For your own information, I have been HIV positive for over five years now."

So, I might now be infected?

With that truth acknowledged, a tear fell on my heated checks. I started crying silently as he continued touching me. He was laughing all the more as I cried, sometimes just chuckling to himself. When he stopped laughing and had calmed down a bit, he said.

"I now want the list, ok?"

I couldn't answer him anymore. I was beyond caring about my life. He already had destroyed my life. Why another session of my confession to add to that?

"Time for small talk is over; where is the list?"

He started shouting at me, telling me that I was a traitor to the

4

national cause because I refused to obey orders; that I had shit on their campaigns to clean the image of the country by lying about things that were not even happening. He said that as he started knocking me with his bunched up fists. For long minutes, he repeatedly knocked me even though I was howling with pain. The blows kept coming, hammering me all over my body until I could only grunt in response to each pummeling.

When he was tired, he rested a bit, for five minutes or so, and then he started on it again, punching me on my face, my head, my stomach, kicking me on my buttocks, slamming his fists on my breasts. I couldn't anymore associate the pain inside me with the blows landing on my body. I was nothing more than simply a welt of pure pain. When he was tired again, he stopped. A couple minutes later, he left without a word.

After about thirty minutes of even some more painful torture, trying to figure out whether he was returning back to torture me some more or not, he returned again, smelling of marijuana smoke. So that's what he had been doing and was still doing. He still had a burning butt of a marijuana cigarette which he was still smoking. This time he didn't say anything, but burnt my body with that butt of marijuana and burnt my clothes. I was now fighting two battles, trying to fight to avoid having my clothes catch fire and trying to avoid the butt from burning my flesh as well. He liked the game and continued this for long moments.

The burning smell of my flesh, the pain all over my body, and the suffocating burn of the marijuana smoke to my lungs, all that was too much for me; I passed out. He left me and when I came to he was back. He returned back with two jugs of water; one of cold water and another of hot water, almost boiling-hot water. He doused me with hot water first and the burning scalding pain! I winced from this pain, and then he doused me in almost freezing water. The pain was indescribable, incomprehensible.

Then, he started stomping on me like a furious elephant. My ribs cracked on my left side. I felt them crashing onto my stomach pit. He also broke my leg, my left arm and, when he was tired again, he simply left without a word. I waited with trepidation of what was coming next. I whimpered with pain for the rest of that afternoon. In the evening, at about seven, he returned back with a water hose which he connected to an outside water tape. Then, he started filling up my cell with cold tap water.

The door to my cell was almost at thigh-level height and he filled it until the water spilled over the rim. It was the middle of a very cold winter, in July, so the combination of this cold water and July's freezing nights froze my cell. Temperatures during that night hit the minus digits. I spent the whole of that night hugging the pole. I hugged the pole, refused to tear myself from it. I gathered myself to the pole, communed with it.

Standing in the freezing waters, breathing with the room! My legs were blocks of ice the following morning. I couldn't even feel them. He ignored me for the rest of that morning. In the afternoon, he came back and took me outside in chains. He took me to the middle of the block of buildings that circled the place around. The cells were tobacco barns which had been turned into torture chambers by these security details.

In the middle of the buildings were all my work mates. They had been tortured as well. They were wearing different kinds of wounds on their bodies. My assistant was the tortured the worst. She was whimpering in pain like me so she had been getting an equal measure of the punishment I had been getting for refusing these pigs a list, a list that didn't even exist. There were about six torturers at the camp I discovered that afternoon. There were some other people other than my office mates who were there, being tortured as well for different kinds of perceived political misdemeanors.

Those pigs said they wanted the list or they were going to kill one of us. They said that we hadn't taken them seriously about the issue. When no list came out, they took my assistant and pushed her onto the ground. They put a heavy metal board on top of her in order to suffocate her, on top of which they added stones in an attempt to extract the list from us. They made us lie face down on the gravel ground with arms out like supine crucifixion. They told us they were going to remove those stones and the board if we were to produce the list. At one point, we tried to lie about where they could get the list thinking they would let her out from under the board and remove the stones. But, when they checked, they couldn't find the list. Failing to find one, they returned back even angrier. They added some more stones on top of her so we stopped lying.

Every day, we were taken to the middle of the blocks of buildings where our workmate was slowly dying. We would watch helplessly as she got flattened by the weight of the stones and the board. The weight of all those stones was too much. It forced her tongue to come out between her teeth. The board and stones flattened her and it took three days of watching for her to die. It was so inhuman having to watch her for those three days as she died.

My assistant had been abducted with her three year old little kid whom she had taken to work with that day because her helping hand had taken some days off to attend a funeral. She failed to arrange for someone to take care of the kid so the kid had been abducted with us. The kid had to cry himself to sleep watching his own mother dying until he couldn't cry anymore. Whenever something is dying it is as if everything else in close proximity also feels the blast of death. Transfixed, we watched her as she expired, as she fought for her last courageous breath, her last string to her humanity.

The pigs had chosen her, a woman barely into her twenties to make an example to us. What they didn't know that day was that they had killed us when they killed her. Now, the slow rush of her death was our revenge. When the dying becomes dead, those left behind in the after-shock continue to live their now half-lives which they first deny are half-lives.

The night she died, he came to my cell and tried to extract the list. When he failed, he ignited my hair on fire. Even though I tried to fight him, I didn't really care anymore what would become of me. My struggle was just an unconscious impulse, automatic. In the aftermath, the biggest chunk of my head was bald and full of lacerations and boils. It felt like my mind was one painful boil. I couldn't think of anything really. I thought my brains were cooked. My nose was broken in several places; my tongue was bitten; and several teeth were broken.

These interrogations continued for several weeks. I lost count of the days, weeks after weeks passed. I could feel my body decaying in some places. I couldn't feel all of my body's limps. Some nights, I had bouts of violent headaches after stormy sessions of vomiting while remembering my rape. Some nights, I was doused with boiling water, sugar and coffee concoctions. He would throw hot cups of coffee onto my face and he would record the volume of my screams on the tape player so that he could determine the decibel levels of the pain he was inflicting on me. This slick sticky scalding mixture would scald my entire body. I got black eyes on other days from the beating. I spent my days and nights caked in layers of caked-on blood all over my body.

One morning, he came and was in such a good mood, whistling to himself, grinning, laughing, and his tongue lolling from a smile that could tear limbs. He told me that we were going to be transferred to the Chikurubi maximum prison to await trial. That day, we were taken to this new torture chamber, but I knew we would be a little protected there. Someone knew we were still alive. Most importantly, we would finally be able to access our lawyer.

Later that day, our lawyer came to see us in the prison. He was shocked to see me wounded that bad. He told me he had been looking for us and that he had to petition the courts to force the Minister of Security to release us into police custody. A couple of weeks later, he managed to have our case referred to the Supreme Court, and the Supreme Court couldn't find a technicality to hide behind in refusing me to seek and see a doctor. After seeing the prison doctor's affidavit stressing the inadequacy of the prison hospital and the necessity of getting me medical attention in a hospital with proper facilities, the court directed that I should receive "appropriate medical attention as a matter of urgency." How appropriate, was still to the determination of the police, and when, was still to the police's discretion.

It was after a week when I was taken, locked in leg irons and under armed escort, to the Avenues Clinic in Harare. I was examined by the doctors, still in leg irons, sent for an x-rays, still in leg irons, and given an ultrasound scan to assess any internal injuries. And, still in leg irons, I was admitted for treatment and was put on a drip. The prison warders still refused to allow me to remain in the hospital and against my will, and still in leg irons, and on the drip; they took me back to Chikurubi. The clinic refused to sign my discharge papers as I was removed against their professional medical advice.

I knew I could take all that now; my mind now worked by funnelling that strange life into dutiful hedgerows to separate me from those who had been damned in the hands of the law. My work mates were later released without a trial, but they kept me saying I had a case to which I must answer. I knew time would heal the beating, but would never heal the pain of the rape and self-disgust. Yet, I had to leave that be, for the hardest part of the game was over.

Chapter 2: THE TORTOISE

There is this story my grandmother told us during one rainy summer night as we surrounded the grate. We were roasting maize cobs and smiling all around. We were celebrating life there, without knowing why. These moments, our family together around the grate, which continue to linger as some of our brightest. It was on that night, she told us the story of a tortoise. It's a story which lingers in my memory as a meditation on, among other things, the momentary nature of an individual life and the timelessness of our human struggle, as part of something larger.

The tortoise once lived in a small pool left off after a long devastating draught in Pungwe River. Five years before, when the water started drying up, all the water animals died, except for this small tortoise. It had survived the drought in a small pool which was slowly drying up. Knowing that this home was no longer hospitable and still very young with a heart of adventure, the tortoise started on a long journey through the craggy, hilly and thorny thick bushes of Nyanga Mountain. Two years on the move saw it into Karombe area, which is now the apple-growing estate of Clairemount. How it had survived that draught; how it had survived without water; how it had covered such a long distance through the thick mountainous forest; what it had survived from through those two years of rainless draughts...no one knew.

Finally, it arrived in Karombe area. The tortoise had given up hope of ever finding water, when one day, still early in the morning with the heat building, he came upon a lot of trees which were wilting. A great many had shaken off their leaves and dried up.

Under one of those trees, our tortoise hid by shuffling under the leaves which were strewn all over the ground. The tortoise hoped to hide from the scorching sun's rays, at least for some few more days.

One by one, one after another, the leaves were falling down from the trees. Our tortoise was finding a temporary respite under the leaves, a shelter from the never-ending draught, a shelter from this long thirsty journey, or maybe a shelter from worrying about what would become of tomorrow.

For five days, it had laid under the tree. It was almost covered by leaves, except for its head which every morning it raised from its sleep-like posture to gaze up at the sky. Why was the tortoise looking up the sky? Was our tortoise counting the number of leaves left on the tree? Was it sending its silent prayers to the powers above? It seemed as if it were meditating, praying. Was it asking for a single droplet of water to fall down and quench its thirst? Yet, despite the tortoise's attention to the sky, for its meditations, for its prayers, there was no sign of any clouds in the clear blue skies. After a minute or so it would lower its head and wait, but for what?

And, grandmother, who told this tale so beautifully, would look at each of us carefully as she worded this question:

"When would this other torture end?"

And, her answer was instant. The sky had opened. Yet, the tortoise couldn't think quite well on what was really happening. All of a sudden, it started sliding, in a flush of runoff water. It poured heavily, as if all the waters of this world had been released all of a sudden. Could these be the rains the world had waited upon? Had our tortoise finally found a watery shelter from the sun? Might our tortoise look forward to a better tomorrow?

But, little did our tortoise know: this was nothing more than a moment. Except for that downpour, it never rained again. Meanwhile, our friend, the tortoise, had fortunately found a friend, another water animal, a skinny-thin frog with dangerously protruding eyes. The thought of a tiny frog egg surviving the long drought in such a desolate place waiting for a moment, a chance, an opportunity to produce a new life boggles our mortal minds. Together, they shared a pool which had gathered, seemingly, just for them.

Unfortunately, this pool was nothing but a temporary rest; he didn't belong here anymore than he had anywhere before this. When the water was almost dry and too hot to live in, when one morning his friend the frog had woken up dead; the tortoise started on another journey down the rolling valleys of Nyatate area. Resigned to the journey, he sniffed the air and began the journey again to a world abundant with water.

"Years later," my grandmother would round out her stories with this preamble, "if you happen to stay in this area you could have seen a craggy, old and barely moving object. That's our tortoise in its journey to a place beyond all those dried rivers. That's our tortoise still moving slowly though. It's been years and it's not near any water, neither is it near the sea."

Chapter 3: ZANZIBAR

He is an adult. He should have been married by now. But, he is always running away when things seems to be settling down, always finding a way to pack his bags and get on the road. It's perpetual, his wandering life is. He is always on the move, perhaps driven insane by the war years not long behind. Yet, even a man as restless as he has been still has a family, someone who listens to his stories.

"Once, during the liberation war years, during the late sixties..."

Uncle always started the stories that way and we would instantly recognize that there was a story about to be told so we would give our rapt attention.

"There was this huge fight with Smith's soldiers in Watsomba..."

We couldn't really ask where Watsomba actually was because we knew this uncle might as well reply that it was in Bindura. We also knew that Bindura wouldn't, in any way, be Watsomba. We had learned the art of listening to the stories without trying to authenticate them.

"There was a fierce battle for a couple of days and all the liberation soldiers were killed, except for me. When I realized I was the only one left, I stopped firing back at Smith's dogs. I knew they would be coming to check whether every soldier had been killed so I took the corpses of the other liberation war soldiers, doused myself with their blood and heaped a couple of those corpses on top of me to mimic someone who was dead. I had to hold my breath closely when Smith's soldiers were checking the corpses. When they were sure all the liberation forces had been killed, including me who they even poked with a rifle to make sure that I was dead, they left us to rot. You know I had to suck the pain without twitching, not even a single muscle of my body. It was hell having to do that, son..."

He would stop at that and just watch the western horizon as if he could see his dead compatriots hanging there, dust in the wind. If, when he told these stories, they were fishing, he would stare into the waters for a long time as if he was seeing that battle happening again in the calm of the river's currents. Later, he would finish the story, speaking as if his soul was echoing up from a deep pit.

"When I knew they had gone for sure, I disentangled myself from those corpses and left Watsomba for Zanzibar."

He always said he left for Zanzibar after that battle, even though the details in the stories evolved during each telling. At the end of the story, he always left for Zanzibar. Zanzibar was always his refuge, the place of redemption, of rebirth.

In another version of the story, he said that, when he had been doused in blood of his compatriots while hiding under them pretending to be dead, he had gone crazy from the smell. In this version, he said that when Smith's soldiers were just paces from him, checking on the dead liberation soldiers, he had shifted his position under his friends dead bodies which still dripped warm blood on him, grabbed his still loaded rifle, and had fired on the unsuspecting soldiers. In this version, he wiped out all of Smith's soldiers. Then, he had left for Zanzibar. It was difficult to know which version was the correct version of this story.

We hadn't known where Zanzibar was and for some years we wouldn't find out. When we got to know where it actually was, we had asked Uncle how he had traveled there. Uncle replied, with a strange look in his eye, that he had walked to Zanzibar.

Zanzibar is an island. How could he have walked across the Indian Ocean?

We knew uncle was lying. We later heard rumors that Uncle hadn't really left for Zanzibar after that battle. Rather, he had stayed in Watsomba, turned into a rogue element, and was stealing from the villagers of this area at gun point. Sometimes, we heard rumors that he had abused the woman in that area. In these rumors, some had even suggested that he had really helped Smith's men to wipe-out the liberators at Watsomba.

After the liberation war, he continued with his drifting ways especially after he retired from the army. He would just leave home without telling anyone. He would drift for months on end and, after some months, he would find his way back home.

He would, of course, tell us stories.

Chapter 4: EATING WHILST RUNNING

My childhood was a torn cloud. It didn't matter what day it was, the war for liberation removed time, but I still remember the day when we were running. My younger brother was beside me and my older brother Bernard was carrying our young sister, Gladys. I was holding his hand. The inside of his skin felt so soft, like water, like I could have fallen through his skin and into him.

On that day, we were drinking tea with the baked maize bread we called, "Chimupoto High." When we saw other people running, we knew nothing good could happen. So, we grabbed our Chimupoto High and the cups of tea and ran to the fields. We were sometimes running, sometimes eating our food on our way to the fields. We had only time for greedy little bites as we scurried from shelter to shelter until we reached the open fields.

Our home had been the political base for the liberators. They stayed and slept in their tents near the gates of our home, near a thorn-infested Mutsotsoti tree, just behind my youngest uncle's Hozi (a traditional bedroom built on top of four big squared boulders of stones, build of dagga, logs and thatched by grass). We knew there was trouble when we saw the liberators packing their guns onto their shoulders and advancing. Their faces gripped; their bodies tensed, focused, locked into battle mode.

We also knew that this meant that we were going to sleep outside that night.

We would always run to the fields, which were open fields where we knew we would be safe from Smith's soldiers who would come into the villages looking for the liberation soldiers. We knew that Smith's soldiers wouldn't venture anymore into the fields because they would be in the open in the fields. They had tried that before; they had come into the fields looking for us. On that night, our family had stayed home. I still don't know how mother knew there was going to be bloodshed in the fields that night. She simply told us we were staying home that night, come-what-may.

That night, the liberators, hiding in the nearby mountains, wiped hundreds of Smith's soldiers in the valleys of Matimba. The liberators had ambushed Smith's soldiers. When Smith's soldiers saw that they were perishing in large numbers, they started firing at the local families who were hiding nearby so as to stop the liberators from firing at them.

Even though we decided to stay home that night, we could not sleep, not even a wink, the whole night, hearing the cluck-cluck-cluck sounds, the thunder and roar of the AK47s, the bazookas, and the grenades. Seeing red arrows of the bullets whizzing south-north in these fields, we watched this dance with hearts that were exploding with fear and trepidation throughout that dark night. In the morning, we were finally able to steal some sleep when the battle had eased.

That morning, we entered the bloodied killing fields to help the liberators bury those three or so family members who had died in that battle and the soldiers on both sides of the camp who we didn't even know who their relatives were. We didn't even have to dig six foot deep graves, no. There was no time for that. We dug deeply enough so that the fallen soldiers wouldn't be exhumed by the dogs. But, of course, these were barbaric times. Some were exhumed by the packs of wild dogs and became their food.

In the afternoon when we returned home, we cooked and ate.

Later, when my grandmother was going to her garden, all hell broke loose again. Smith's soldiers had come down through Nyajezi River without being detected. We were hit unprepared this time. They attacked our home where I suppose someone had told them the liberators were based. That afternoon, I got caught in the line of crossfire for the first time. I was young, about five or six. It felt like it was happening in another world. Things seemed like they were frozen in time, almost as in a surreal dream. I felt cut off from everything, yet somehow in the center of everything. It was a vortex.

When we heard the first gun shout, we snuck into the hedges to the north of our yard perimeter. Momma and the four of us squeezed into the hedges which separated our home from Cousin Michael's home. We ran deep into the hedges, a bit down from our home. We hid there with his family. We got to the cattle kraals which were a bit down, a bit removed from the battle lines. At the kraals, we sought shelter in the goat's pen. That's when we saw our grandmother straggling, running on her way back home, moving though the middle of the crossfire. We called her to come to the kraals which were a bit safer, but she ignored us.

Grandmother kept running like some demented person who was possessed of some spirit. She was right there in the middle of the killing fields, but she wasn't afraid. That day, I realized how strong and strange my grandmother was.

She started singing very loudly. We didn't know the words to the song so her singing sounded as if she was humming to a song, but she was actually singing so loud. No one knew the words. It was in a language we had never heard of before; in fact, there was no such language. She later told us that she didn't even know she was singing at that moment. She couldn't remember the melody or the words. But, she said, if she was really singing, then the slow and tragic sadness of the moment had moved through her and had vibrated across her vocal chords. It was one of those strange experiences which so beautifully characterize our humanity amidst the calamity of war.

Beholding her, both sets of the fighters stopped firing at each other. I think they were surprised, seeing an old lady running across the battle lines singing a strange song as if there was no care in the world for her. We were scared as shit knowing that this moment, this unearthly pause, and our dear grandmother could abruptly end; all that was needed was just a single bullet. She would be dead. We held our breath. Watching her, bewitched and entranced, we were maybe scared as well. It wasn't until she had arrived home and had stopped singing when the battle resumed again into the night.

We stayed inside those goat's pens until it was dark. Momma snuck back home through those hedges, and collected some cooking things. She returned back with my grandmother and our youngest uncle, who was my grandmother's last child. Grandmother later told us that he was the reason why she had risked her life; she wanted to see that her son was fine. Together, as a family, we left home, went down to the river and followed the Nyajezi River down to the north into the next village, Gwanyan'wanya village. It was far removed from the fighting and battle lines. We stayed at Mai Sabina Nyabocho's residence, sleeping outside for a week until the fighting had died down in our village.

A week later, when we returned back to our village, our homes had been razed to the grounds and the liberation forces had disbanded into the nearby mountains. We had to sleep outside for some couple of weeks as we got the roof of the kitchen, which still had standing walls, up again. Throughout the following two weeks, we also buried the soldiers from both sides of the camps, some of whom were already rotting around the perimeters of our home.

Even now, our home is surrounded by a lot of graves of these unknown soldiers from both sides whose life was ended during that fierce battle. The sadness still lingers in the streams, lands, forests and vast mountains around our homes. The area is still haunted by spirits and ghosts of the liberation struggle.

We had to run a couple more times after that, but both times didn't amount to much because Smith's soldiers were now afraid of coming into the villages which they knew were well protected by the liberators. We didn't stay that long out in the fields both of those times. One of those times, the whole village had to sleep outside, near our fields. By then, though, I don't remember running with my younger brother. I don't remember his hand in mine.

For years, I have thought to myself that he must have died in one of those battles, only to be told later when I had gathered enough courage to ask my mother about him, that he had died from a different cause. As it turns out, all those times I thought I was running with him, his hand in mine, he was already dead of pneumonia, not of the bullets. I couldn't have argued with my mother about it. I couldn't have told her that I felt him next to me during all those days and nights we were running from Smith's soldiers.

Even today, when I think of him, I only remember those days when we were running together, avoiding the red-arrow bullets. No bullets hit either of us, but it still feels as if a bitter splinter of the bullets flicked its metal spine and crossed through time to remind me of him.

It was on one of those two other times when we had to sleep outside in the fields when, early in the morning, we saw our uncle and my father's cousin coming to us. We had to run into the woods, almost everyone had scurried away into the woods thinking that the two had become Smith's informers and were leading Smith's soldiers to wipe us out. It turned out that the two had been captured by Smith's soldiers a couple of months before. We trickled back to our makeshift camp slowly when we didn't see Smith's soldiers following them. That day, we celebrated their release and the end of the war.

They had brought the good news to us, that the war had been stopped to allow for the negotiations that were ongoing in a foreign land known as Britain, at Lancaster house. It was early 1979 then. They told us they had been released as a sign of goodwill. That day, we killed a big bull, cooked, and bathed for the first time in ages. We ate, celebrated, and caroused. The end of the war had happened. We were finally going to stop running, to be free, to eat food in our homes, and to adopt normal lives.

We looked forward to go back to the schools that had been closed for a year now, as the fighting had been too out of control. During that year, we had witnessed the night of red arrows, nights spent outside sleeping under the sky, under the unblinking stars. We knew that the days of running away from Smith's soldiers, and eating food whilst running had ended. On that night, we ran. We ran, not from something, but towards something. We ran towards a future which held promise.

Chapter 5: GUKURAHUNDI

Over 20 000 died and the mounting death toll kept mounting...

I was a little boy of about seven years old. I was at the kraals about to take the goats and cattle to the graze lands when I saw the Puma army vehicles coming into our village. I knew it meant trouble. The fearsome fifth brigade had been deployed in our area. We had heard news about them from the other villages of Filabusi. They hadn't been to our village before. Our village was a low vibe village. But in all the villages they had been to, only a few had survived to tell the story. They were said to be wiping out whole villages. Gukurahundi meant simply that: the wiping out of whole villages.

When I saw them and their vehicles, I took cover in the gulley near our kraals. It was simply a survival instinct, I should think. I watched as they collected the whole village. They collected the whole village as if we were nothing but dried cow dung (hundi in Gukurahundi) for burning. It wasn't difficult to do that because our village was close knit, almost a high density suburb. They took everyone to just beyond our cattle kraals, near the village burial site. They took my father, my mom, and my two little sisters as well. I followed behind them, but still under cover.

Our leaders, Joshua Nkomo, Ndumiso Dabengwa, and others had been waging a recalcitrant war against Mugabe's alienation politics on the Ndebele people. The war had been going on for nearly two years. It was in 1985, about October. For those two years, we hadn't seen or had been caught in the crossfire. Only about two or so weeks before that fateful day, they had started ransacking our Filabusi area. Up till then, the war had been concentrated in the Matebeleland north province, in the Lupane area. They were many rebels there. Most of the political leaders of ZANLA party, the mother body of the ZIPRA rebels who had been waging this war, also came from Matebeleland, just north of our region.

At the gravesites, they accused the villagers of protecting Gwesira and the rebels who were fighting this recalcitrant war. The villagers denied the allegations, saying that they had neither seen any rebels nor fed any of them. But, this argument didn't last long. The notorious fifth brigades shot a couple of people to show they meant business. They told the villagers to start digging a huge hole for their burial. Nobody in his right frame of mind could have gone against this command.

I watched as the people started digging their own grave using their own hands, sometimes with sticks or stones to help them. I saw my family among them. I could see the terror on their faces and the blood on their hands. Those soldiers watched, unimpressed in the face of this humanity.

Our village was a sizable village of over thirty households. At the grave site, nearly two hundred of my closest relations cowered together against the fifteen armed-to-the-teeth soldiers. There was nothing they could have done. There was nothing I could have done, either. I couldn't get out of my hiding place because I knew it meant instant death. So, I watched them digging their own grave. For over three hours, they had labored on and dug a huge hole that was deep enough and big enough to accommodate the whole village.

At about mid afternoon, the soldiers told the villagers to stand by the mouth of the grave, five at a time. Five soldiers stood there at a time, as well. I heard them as they asked the villagers to tell them where the rebels were. I heard them warn my people that, if they kept quiet, then they would shoot and you would fall into the grave. They were clear that, if anyone lied, they would shoot you. They all knew that, even if they told the truth, there was only one end to this moment. Each would collapse into the grave, life after life wasted.

The other ten soldiers were securing and guarding the place. It was difficult to keep track of the killing. I simply died inside watching, but I still watched. I knew that these brave people deserved to be witnessed by something more than the evil of the moment. That afternoon, they wiped almost the whole village, pushed everyone into the grave, even those who were still alive, including the helpless and innocent children of our village. I was the only one saved.

I don't even remember seeing them killing my family, but I knew they were killed. No one escaped. When every person was inside this grave, they took the shovels from their Puma army trucks and started covering the grave with the soil and stones. Some people were buried alive. It should have taken them a couple or so hours to bury my village. I hadn't waited to watch that. I just couldn't wait anymore. I walked away into the next village, and the next, and the next. I drifted southwards. I kept walking for days on end, ate whatever I could get from the bushes or from other villages. I just wanted to get as far away as was possible from those killing fields.

How I survived, I don't even know. Many villages other than

ours were also cleansed in those years. Many people were buried alive in mass graves in the Matabeleland region.

I grew up in Gwanda town, adopted by a childless family in this town. I told them I was Sibusiso. They adopted everything, except my heart that had died that October day. I couldn't refuse to feel this way the way the sky feels nothing, not even the blue of itself. My heart had fallen, buried into the earth like what happened to my village.

Chapter 6: MUSHAZHIKE

At the end of 2003, late on a Sunday afternoon, we left for Mushazhike. There were four of us in our little gang: my niece; my friend, Joseph; my niece's friend, Mai Magobo; and me. We had heard that there was some illegal gold mining happening deep in the commercial farming communities of Concession at a place known as Mushazhike. Thinking that a bit of fortune awaited us there, we became part of the horde that was providing trade to these people, these illegal miners, who were far removed from the nearest trading centre.

People had developed a tent city there and were bringing basic commodities for trade. These illegal panniers sold their gold to illegal gold dealers who were also there, hanging about, hoping to snatch up any little nugget which might emerge from the Earth. Mai Magobo had colored everything in bright colours, or maybe it was my niece who did that. My niece had a talent at that, too. Joseph and I thought we were going to do a roaring trade.

My internal world was ready for a change of fortune. A couple of weeks before, I had awakened one morning and had futilely looked for food in the dry kitchen. There was nothing to scrounge in the room; so, I drew back the curtains to close them, made the room dark again, and told myself it wasn't yet time for breakfast. Even when I knew and could see the sun peeping through the curtains, I told lies to myself that it wasn't yet morning.

The edges of hunger were already nibbling at the edges of my ribs. I worked hard to lie to myself that it was still night for as long as possible. When my hunger became a tick biting into the resilient flesh of my stomach, and fearing that one day I would never wake up from this perpetual hunger, I woke up from the lie and went to the industrial centre to look for work, just a day's job that might afford me some food.

Luck was on me; I found a job which lasted a week. At the end of that week, I took the wages and bought some things to trade at Mushazhike. The pain of hunger was no longer there. That hungry belly, the nibbling tick, was distant, located somewhere else. The hunger forgotten, the impulse driving me was now this theory that I could create a trading concern. The fledgling impulse for entrepreneurship gained ground within me, no thanks to my niece and Mai Magobo.

With the wages, we procured cigarettes, beer and wine to trade through Joseph's connections at the illegal gold mines. We hurriedly prepared our things while our fortune, awaiting us in Mushazhike, danced in our minds. At least, it did in mine. Clothes and various items were quickly strewn across our rooms as we rushed to meet these eagerly-anticipated fortunes. The good thing was that it was in December, midsummer almost, so we didn't need a lot of blankets. We had only one for the two of us; one for Joseph and me and the ladies had one, as well.

Impatient to get to our future, we spent the extra cash and took a taxi to Concession in Leopold Takawira Street, instead of riding the bus. It was mostly an uneventful journey, except for the one moment during that journey during which our taxi stopped to add another fare. Before the turn-off to Concession from Bindura Road, there was this scraggy, dirty woman who flagged for the taxi. The driver picked her up. She smelled so bad. Worse, she knew it. The guilt was palpable. She hid from us.

The new rider was so dirty and looked so old, even though she was still obviously young. In her late twenties, I thought. She looked like someone in her fifties or sixties, so worn down by life in those farming areas. That's what staying and working in farm lands does to you, I couldn't help thinking. She sat by my side. I had to suck it up. Lucky for me, she didn't travel with us for long, though. It seemed everyone, including the driver, breathed a sigh of relief when she disembarked from the taxi.

From Concession, we took some old beaten trucks that were doing a roaring trade transporting all manner of things into the deep farmlands of Mushazhike. It was only a distance of ten to fifteen kilometers, yet they were charging the same fares we had paid from Harare which was some sixty kilometers away. There was no competition for those trucks. There were not more than five trucks doing that trade at that time. That was a market which was easy to control. The place they were plying was basically underdeveloped, with eaten-out dusty roads.

We were packed, twenty of us or so, in a single one ton truck. We had no choice; there was nothing else that could take us there. The ride was truly brutal; we were all shaken to within an inch of death by vomit. The only saving grace was the air moving past, which also deposited a thick layer of dust across our faces and exposed skin. It was only moments before we were as dirty as the young lady in the taxi, even if we didn't yet smell as bad.

They dumped us in some kind of central place. This drop-off point was just outside some old rundown property. There was still some kind of broken wall of some sort around the property. I thought we were lost somehow because outside of those walls there were just some few people taking lifts back to Concession. Yet, when we entered that farm's gates, I got the surprise of my life.

Before us, there were the remains of the farm's buildings and a barn. But, to the west and to the south, was what looked to be a thriving market town, though without tap water, shelter, or any creature comforts. Instead, there were thousands of people trading all sorts of things, all lured here with the same promise of fortune dancing. These were my people, my fellow countrymen: desperate, yet full of hope.

There were those trading food things, cooking food, selling mining implements, exhibiting clothes, hawking electrical gadgets, and those peddling cigarettes, beer and wine like what we had planned on doing. For the three days we were there, it was written in the newspapers afterward that over 10,000 people were there or passed through that place. The place was packed and had all the signs of a roaring trade. When we arrived, though, no one was buying anything.

"So, where are the buyers, Mai Magobo?"

"Oh, don't worry, Uncle. They will be coming by night's fall. They are in the fields just there."

She turned and pointed into the woods to the north. I thought to myself she was simply trying to encourage us. There was nothing we could see that far from where we were, so I asked her.

"How many, roughly, are out there?"

"Many, especially these days...They say there are so many illegal panniers this side. The police have been lenient and the illegal panniers have been getting better output from their holes, as well."

I also wondered what their mines looked like, so I asked her.

"How do they mine their stones?"

"They dig deep holes into the soil. There is not much alluvial mining happening here so they have to work some real hard digging down."

"Alluvial, huh?"

"Yes, Uncle, there's no water here."

I laughed silently at her use of the word 'alluvial' when so much of her vocabulary was the course patois of the street. At the same time, though, I marveled at the thought of spending my days digging a big hole in the dusty ground with just the hopes of a tiny nugget of gold to motivate me from shovel load to shovel load. I thought to myself, this must be some difficult work!

We rested from our journey under some trees near the trading place. The trading place was a strip road, running a little over the dimension of a street's width and length. We took our spot along this strip by spreading a plastic on top of the red clay and displaying our things. The traders would walk through this strip, looking at both sides of the strip for the things they wanted to buy.

All that afternoon, I had been meaning to empty my bowels, but didn't know where to go. I hadn't seen anyone going to the toilet or accessing one. I was ashamed of asking my niece's friend, Mai Magobo. By night's fall, I could barely contain myself any longer. Not able to take the pressure anymore, I asked her, as politely as possible, where I could empty my bowels. Luckily, she couldn't see the embarrassment on my face on this thankfully dark, December night.

She told me I could go to the west, some distance into the bush. I thanked her and disappeared quickly, furtively, desperately into the blackened gullet of the night. Thirty meters into the bush, I saw a girl, who had the same idea, helping herself and knew that it was a good enough distance. Embarrassed, I found another spot a couple or so meters away which would serve my purpose fine.

As I squatted there and reflected on this crazy situation, vivid memories of some years before when we went to Botswana with my niece, her husband, another niece and a band of other friends to trade things there came flooding back to me. Instead of December, the trip to Botswana had been in January, almost five years before. Those January days in Botswana were perpetual sunsets, always apocalyptic, with the Sun on one side, big, hot, and bright, and sweltering dark air on the other!

On that occasion, we had stayed in White City, a small suburb just at the edges of Gaborone city centre. We were selling clothing that time. We had to sleep outside; the homes couldn't have accommodated the hundreds of us. I remembered I had to spend some couple of weeks at that time in that place sleeping on the ground with a blanket, counting the stars in the clear, beautiful, yet uninterested Botswana skies, hoping that the shoppers would find some value in my wares.

The only breeze in Botswana was generated from the wings of the mosquitoes sipping on our blood. We hadn't slept really; every moment was the key to our commercial success that time. The only difference with Mushazhike was that Gaborone was a town, a city, a village or whatever it was. In Botswana, at least, we had access to some clean tap water there, though the toilets and bathrooms were not by any stretch better. There, the cesspit toilets had to be drained. When we arrived, they were already bursting with shit, bubbling out, and flowing away as nasty raw sewage.

The bathrooms were so dirty that we preferred to create a dense wall of bodies into a circle to block passers-bye so that they couldn't see us. We would take turns to get a quick bath in the middle of that circle. It had to be a quick job. At the time, we thought Botswana was a primitive hell. Now, here in Mushazhike there were no baths to talk of, no toilets, nothing. We had devolved; we had descended back to the cave age. This was worse. Civilization was just a memory here, something to trade stories about between swatting flies and noisily wheezing through dusty throat-choking breaths of stale air.

When I had finished emptying my bowels and stumbled back into the market area, the others were already asleep. I settled in and took the first shift guarding our things that night. We had been warned that thieves were stealing everything they could lay their hands on. There were no rules, no laws at this place. Nothing was sacred. Wives were taken from their husbands without a by-your-leave, as quickly and rampantly as the goods the traders had brought there in an effort to turn a profit. I slept at twelve that night when Mai Magobo took over for her two to three hours of watching over our things.

Early the following morning, we bought boiled water, a cup each for the four of us for about $2.00US each. We brought with us some tea leaves and sugar so we made tea which we drank with stale bread which was sold by another among the crowd there. After breakfast, we displayed our things again, trading to the early morning customers. A couple of our things were picked up. It was so slow, so painfully slow, such that by about nine that morning we had traded very little, not even enough to afford us all a day's worth of food.

"Mai Magobo, we don't seem to be selling much?" Joseph asked my niece's friend.

"Yes, there seem to be a lull this time." She concurred, but encouraged us with a few positive words. "Things will definitely pick up. It's still the start of the week. The more they get the stones from their holes, the more they would have spare money to buy a bit. Let's hold on a bit, guys."

We nodded our heads in agreement, still hoping for our fortune to appear. But, before long, we saw people running into the bushes. We couldn't wait to ask why. It meant the police were around. Last night, one of the neighbours had warned us of this. So, we grabbed our things and made for the forest to the Northwest where there was a small knoll of a hill.

When we got to the top of it, we stopped running and looked back at the market place. From there, we could see the police busily putting those they had captured into their three Defender patrolling vehicles. A couple more minutes after, they left for the nearest police station, the one at Concession. Nothing was left behind, but another gritty dust cloud.

We weren't too worried about the situation, though. We all knew that, if you get caught all that you had to do was bribe those police off at Concession so that you won't be brought before the courts and be fined bigger fines than what the police were taking. It seemed that everyone connected to Mushazhike was entertaining an entrepreneurial spirit.

We waited until when we saw a lot of other people trickling back to the market place. When we returned, we were feeling fairly impatient. By about eleven in the morning, Joseph and I took our trade into the mining areas in the woods to the north, a kilometer or so from the market place. As we were traversing this place, I realized how sore my neck had become from staring at the ground as I walked. I hung a comment into the thick midday air as a warning.

"Friend, this place is now a death trap to the wild animals or stray cattle. There are so many holes here."

The whole place had been desecrated. Barren crates, holes, dilapidated shacks were all over this place. The nearby stream had been flooded by sand and was blocked here and there. The land that should have been used for crop or cattle farming was now consumed by these illegal activities. Joseph laughed at my warning and shared a deliciously barbaric thought with me.

"Yes, I heard that even the illegal panniers are enjoying getting a lot of fresh meat from their holes, as well. This other pannier was saying they were having fresh meat almost every day from animals that died after falling into these holes."

"Do you see that even that stream is blocked and covered in sand? They say it used to flow all year round. Now, it only flows after a flood."

"Yes, I heard that too friend. The desecration of the land is so bad. I heard the owner of the farm was chased out by Joseph Chinotimba."

"Seriously, Chinotimba was here?" I couldn't help asking him.

"Yes, he took the farm right across I am told. They say the white owner of this farm, named Viljoen or something left for South Africa with nothing."

"Stripped of everything like a dog, you mean."

"Yeah, like a dog, my friend."

"The war veterans are said to be stationed at the next farm to the north. They looted everything in this farm, destroyed the farm buildings, and then left for the next farm. Just see how bad this place now looks, friend."

"It's a sad thing, my friend, but let's not waste our time

mourning things that we can't solve anymore. A lot of things are sad and sore in our country these days, even our sad excuses for lives, Tendai!"

"Yes, let's try to sell the things and beat our tracks out of this godforsaken place."

"Tendai, do you think we are going to get much from this endeavor. I don't seem to be sensing the smooth profit business the ladies talked of."

"It's my feeling as well, Jose. But, let's see a day or two here and see what will become of this."

"Yes." Joseph nodded and I looked at him and we exchanged these looks with the same thoughts attached to them. The thought which had seared across our frontal lobes transmitted electrically, synchronously: maybe we are always meant to be losers in life.

Nothing we had done or tried to do in our lives developed into much of anything. Whilst other young people were getting better jobs, whilst some were moving out of the country to better countries like the UK, and whilst still others were continuing with their education, our lives were passing us by in godforsaken Mushazhike, doing nothing much worth talking of, besides dodging trash, gaping holes in the ground, and bemoaning what had become of our beautiful country.

And, even in this depressive state, there was still ways to make things worse. That afternoon, the northern sky acted threatening, but we never minded it. We were already wrapped in the drama of our own depressing existences. In our state of stripped away civility, that same sky was as meek as a newborn in the morning. It was a thinly grey, almost chewy-grey. It had given the impression of a somber kind of joy. It was the quintessential expression of our inner world; yet, we paid it no mind. Instead, we clung to whatever success we could make from this forlorn place, this desperate business.

We visited several holes, got some cigarettes picked up. Other than that, there was little else to convince us of the value of our journey there, or in the value of the life we had been trying to eke.

By about two o'clock, we left for the giant makeshift market place. Our story of little trading was the same story shared by the ladies. Luckily for her, Mai Magobo had cleared a bit of her stuff. She had food things so she had a good market for her food. The panniers had to eat. It was easier for them to abstain from things like cigarettes, but not from food.

The sky was almost pale-blue when we arrived at the market place, saturated with heat. The rain clouds were starting on the western sky. They had a brooding quality; a thickening look about them like something was stirring and turning over in the sky's stormy mind. We noticed that, a bit to the north, the sky was still creamy pink-yellow. To the east, it was a thick purple-grey, darkening. The sky looked like trouble, trouble with a capital T.

The whole atmosphere oozed with something essentially elemental. The sky had been giving enough warning throughout the day. Even if we had spent considerable energy in our self-absorption, the thick clouds had been bunching up together all afternoon, hanging about and muttering the way clouds do. Something resolved up there, though. The temperature plummeted by late afternoon.

Even though we noted this with a single statement, everyone knew that each and every other person at this place was praying silently, once the temperature unzipped us from our funk, that it wouldn't rain that night. Silence descended upon the place, a kind of contemplative silence, a prayer. I tried to remain unconcerned, but those clouds had drifted badly into twisted shapes. Our voices tangled in the dark winds. Could I have prayed to these impending rains those prayers that we seldom pray even though we know all their words? Could I have spoken some magical word unspeaking the venom of my life's suffering? Would the weather listen? Would it care?

That evening, we displayed our stuff, but without much hope. By nightfall the western skies started darkening with real storm clouds. The clouds bunched up like fists ready to strike, dark like the shadows of our thoughts, violent like the impulses in our hearts. The sky was almost thick green-grey with rains about to lower on us. In the distance, the thunder cried. Nearer and nearer the thunder came, until a warning flash of lightning crackled across the impossibly green clouds. Another jerked, flash arching across the sky and, faster now, another struck close to where we were. The sky talked no sense at all, but filled every molecule of my being with terror.

The horizons opened and the rains came crashing down. The thunder growled and the lightening charged a deeper purple-grey as the sky pour down onto the tents, the trees, the land and on us humans. For a moment, it paused as if it was catching its breath, then the deluge exploded down onto all of us. Nature is always nature and nobody controls it. So, the sky oozed out big, stormy, fat, Highveld raindrops.

We put our things inside the plastic and placed our bundles into the trees so that they wouldn't be soaked, soiled, and ruined by the rains. The lightning illuminated everything in a momentary bright pink which seared our eyeballs. There was only one place left for us there, out in the rain. The thunder growled and growled with the halitosis of a giant; our noses twitched. The air had an acrid, metallic smell after every flash of lightning. Out in the open, we faced the storm there, small, insignificant, and still hopeful.

It rained hard for over three hours, until midnight. No one slept anywhere in the encampment that night. We didn't take duties to guard the things that night because we were all awake. The water level rose on the land, moving and flowing northerly to the stream. The stream swelled. The tents were uprooted and small trees were bowled over. We stood on our feet, resisting these widening puddles, and the nasty things which floated by, too. Our minds were busy as we braved the rain still looking for our slice of success in this nowhere of Mushazhike.

The rains kept falling slowly as the night showered into daylight. Hour by hour, the drops of rain became colder. We were subhuman there. We were shaking reeds in the middle of a flooding river, devoured by sleep, riddled with exhaustion. By the time the showers drifted away at about seven in the morning and the sun fisted its way out of the rainy clouds, we spent a couple more hours just trying to let the sun warm us a bit and chase away the gnawing lost feeling feasting deep in our guts. We changed our clothes for the dry ones that we had protected with the plastic. Huddling together for the sun's warmth with the blanket wrapped around us, Joseph and I held each other without shame, just trying to cling to whatever civility we could find in this god-awful and primitive place.

We were two of our own kind, Joseph and I. I loved him. I knew he loved me too. He was the only one of my friends I could still really relate to. All the other friends that I made in my life had drifted away, married, and had fantastic careers. I was still at the same point in my life. It was disheartening, my situation was. It wasn't because of lack of trying, no. I had tried almost everything and nothing had come up good. I envied Joseph, for he still had nine years ahead of him to deal with the things that I was dealing with and to reach my colossal level of failure. I also knew the confirmation of a successful career might never really come for him, as well.

My problem was because of my failure at the "O" level English exam. I failed it a couple more times after the first take. I rewrote it a year after I failed it on my first take and also five years down the line. Maybe I lacked the brush, sun-kissed confidence of my school friends. I had very good passes in all the other subjects at the "O" level, some passes at "A" level as well, but couldn't get any job without English at the "O" level. I couldn't proceed with my studies and do a tertiary course without "O" level English, as well. It was simply a prerequisite in everything I thought I could do with my life.

I had been forced to accept failure on that. Even though I knew it was me standing in my own way, blocking myself. I wasn't able to do anything about it. Failure had become my life, a form of life that was nearest to imperfection. I could feel everything inside me, not just the present-me, but forever-me, my entire past and future. I just felt like a witness to my own life. When I had to spend that whole night awake facing a Highveld storm and deluge, I couldn't help thinking about all that. After all, I would not have had to stand all night in those growing puddles of Mushazhike if I had just been more successful with my English skills.

That day, Joseph and I tried, once we warmed up, to push our things a bit harder, but there was nothing happening. Deeper down, we knew the rains had sapped and washed away whatever spirit and strength we had. We were now just going through the motions. The showers kept coming for a few minutes at a time throughout the day. Most of the day, we spent a lot of time trying to play hide and seek with those showers. By about late afternoon, a wild and freezing cold wind sprouted as if from nowhere, pushing itself on us. The cold front charged through our ranks, rushing winter upon us. It was a wild creature, whipping at us, biting into us, shoving us as if it wanted to bowl us out of our existence.

A few drowsy crickets were warbling, rubbing nearby. Sensitive from our exhaustion, the crickets hypnotized us with their chirping. I found myself melting into the sound until I understood what they were saying over and over, a mantra repeated a thousand million times over and over: "You-are-a-failure, you-are-a-failure, you-are-a-failure." The realization still hurts that even the lowly crickets of Mushazhike were made a tool of my self-discovery. "You-are-a-failure, you-are-a-failure, you-are-a-failure."

The wind kept blowing the cold and wet onto us, gripping handfuls of the landscape as it lunged from one valley to another, one tree to another, one human being to another! That night, it didn't rain, but the ground was freezing from all that rain. That night, we dealt with the cold, with a summer-falsifying winter. I believe the temperatures must have dropped near zero. That night, I cried silently as I shivered from the cold while doing my two hours of guard duty. The others didn't slept for the entire night, either. I could hear them sniffing and sneezing from the cold.

Later, I wrapped into the blanket and tried to penetrate the black exterior around me, but was rewarded with another sleepless night. I gazed into the darkness, at the twinkling stars in the black sky. Thankfully, sleep stole me for an hour between six and seven in the morning. When I woke up, at about half past seven, everyone was awake.

I looked at my friend, Joseph. He was so low-down that he couldn't hold my gaze. My niece looked troubled, to say the least. Even Mai Magobo had some shadows on her face, as well though she looked exactly like the early bird that catches the worm, smug. I noticed that she was almost through selling her stuff. A thought dawned on me and I didn't like it much; I couldn't have voiced it. I felt she had misled us and hadn't told us the truth about what was really moving fast, about what would sell in this godforsaken place. Judging by the few comments between them, I could tell that even my niece wasn't happy with her friend.

Mai Magobo finished selling her things at about half eight in the morning and left for Chitungwiza without even a sympathetic word to us. Joseph and I stayed behind for a couple more hours, visited some holes and sold nothing that day. When we returned to the market place, we told my niece that we were going home that afternoon.

"Stay for a little bit, guys. Things are bound to improve, I tell you!"

"No, we can't take this any longer." I replied with all of the clarity and honesty in my weary heart.

"Uncle, are you going to leave me alone in this bush?" She tried to use guilt to persuade me to stay. But, I wanted nothing to do with it.

"We can go home together if you want, Niece, but it should be now. If you want to stay behind, there is nothing I can do about it. I don't want to leave you behind, but I can't keep pretending things will improve here."

"It's alright, Uncle, but please tell my family that I am okay and that I will be home by the weekend."

I promised her I would do that.

That afternoon, we left Mushazhike for the last time. We left that place with a lot of hard feelings for Mai Magobo for waylaying us, with hard feelings for the illegal gold panniers, who were desecrating the farmlands for less than a handful of gold, with hard feelings for the police, for the summer Highveld rains and the storm, for the shitty realities of our lives.

To sap the anger we had for this place, we decided to walk the anger out to the jumbo shops some 10 or so kilometers from Mushazhike. We were told we could get some lifts to Mazowe from there. We also reasoned we could save a bit on the little we had. That afternoon, we traversed through these commercial farming lands on tired feet.

This area has one of the finest soils in Zimbabwe, a mixture of black, grey, red clay soils which are so rich in nutrients such that one doesn't have to put artificial fertilizers as a supplement of nutrients for the crops. But not even a single farm was cultivated, even though it had been raining well that year. Not even Chinotimba's farm. There was only dust to beat from our feet. Our wits were as bleak and barren as that land. There was no crop to harvest, but misery, that year. This reinforced the feelings that I already had about the much-hyped land reform programme in Zimbabwe.

We have not returned back to Mushazhike, but I have paid

attention over the years to what has become of that place. Nowadays, if you travel through any road out of Harare into the rural communities, all that you can see are vast tracts of fallow farm lands abandoned, misused, and mismanaged by the so-called New Farmers. It's no wonder that Zimbabwe has had to import food ever since the farm invasions. All that this land reform programme meant was that, not only were young people like Joseph and I going to have to deal with the normal difficulty of discovering our adult existence, but also that we would have to contend with years of hunger.

This gaping maw of famine is all over the farmlands, even on the people's faces today. All those promises from the government that we will never go hungry were as empty as my stomach on that morning before I became resolved to face that dark night in Mushazhike. All of the promises they made that we will never be homeless were nothing. Even now, so many years later, we still are.

Chapter 7: BREAKING THE SILENCE

They came to get us in the middle of the night. There was a bad knock on the door. I froze. My husband froze too, the hairs on his hands sprouting up like single black wires curling. We were scared so we waited thinking that maybe our fears were unfounded, that this was all some kind of accident. They called us by our names, telling us to open the doors. We didn't know their voices. There were many voices, some even laughing. In those days, people were disappearing even in broad daylight. We had known all along that there were reprisals even for people who were not MDC supporters. Even those who had ZANUPF party cards disappeared, too. Everyone was fair game so long as you didn't know the new party slogans for ZANUPF, and the only way to learn was to attend the rallies. There was terror everywhere and fear of terror. To even attend the rallies didn't protect you from terror because the situation was simply ungovernable.

The night they came knocking was a very brisk June night; a small bitterly cold wind blew in off the river. We thought we could just ignore them and then they would go thinking that there was no one, but they began to threaten to burn us inside the house. We knew they were going to do that so we opened the doors, scared of what we were going to experience that night. The next neighbor was nearly two hundred metres away so we knew no one would come to help us. They wouldn't even hear us. Even if they were to hear us, we also knew they would never come and put their own lives in danger too.

We discovered a triangle of terror outside: the uniformed police, ZANUPF, and the military. The gang leader was an ugly brute. The second in command was a jackal with a jerk-ass grin, smiling as if he had spotted the day's sport. He bobbed his head up and down in agreement with his leader like the obedient dog that he was. They ordered my husband to carry all the chairs, table, sofas, bed, blankets and clothes, even those that we were wearing were striped from us, and put everything in one room. I had to help him even though I was fully pregnant and was expecting any day.

They took all our food and the cash we had, but for the car. Then, they set fire to all our property and the car. With the burning of all our property, the last fragments of hope that had protected us vanished completely. Our hearts were heavy and sad; our wits numbed as though we were bewitched; our bodies were unable to function; even the tears trickling down our cheeks retained a stunned silence.

They accused us of supporting the opposition MDC party, which we were not even members of. MDC was a forked tongue, an unutterable answer, a snake which would bite you. We had stayed clear of it. They demanded our membership cards, which we didn't have. We thought we would avoid the possibility of this happening to us by not owning any party's cards. Misery was now whispering over and over what a bad mistake we had done by not having those cards, though we also knew that having them wouldn't necessarily have rescued us from this inevitability.

Then, they shot my husband in the legs several times. When I tried to plead with them, they started shouting insults at me. They raised my husband to a metre level height and spread him, holding him suspended in the air. After preparing him thus, they started beating him on his naked buttocks and underneath his feet with large sticks, belts and gun butts. The more he bellowed, the more they pounced on him, until he collapsed. Then, they started in on me.

I told them I was pregnant. They told me I should not have any children. They said that the whole of Zimbabwe would be better off without life. And, secretly, in this moment in the face of this terror, this monstrosity of patriotism, I agreed. They hit me with those sticks, gun butts, belts...on my stomach. The child I was carrying broke into pieces inside my stomach. The baby girl died inside me. Though my husband died that night, it was God's desire that I did not die too.

It was at the hospital that my beautiful child was extracted. The doctors had to cut my stomach to remove those pieces. A head alone, then a leg, an arm, the body..., piece by piece, the rain, the tears of pain...

Chapter 8: NYADZONYA

The week after Mushazhike, I was a bit down with some flu or cold for days. It was a bit bad for the first two days, but as we entered the weekend I was getting better and better. I still had many cartons of cigarettes and bottles of wine left from our wasted Mushazhike endeavor. I decided to take a business trip to Mozambique, to Nyadzonya in Mozambique. Going to trade in Mozambique was the latest sensation. I decided to join the trend of those many entrepreneurs who were already plying this route and opportunity. It was better than sitting around starving, waiting until I got a crack at something worthwhile. I borrowed some money from my sister and from another friend to buff up my stuff, as well as for transport to Nyamaropa and for food on my journey.

Nyamaropa is on the border of Mozambique, in the eastern highlands of Zimbabwe. Mushazhike had been hard work and Nyadzonya meant as much. For some, it had exhausted all the resources of fate. Most people don't have the stamina to be that unlucky and still have the burning passion that I still had inside me to make a success of my life, to push things a bit. Staying at home was still unthinkable for me.

I left Chitungwiza on a Sunday, a week or so before Christmas. I took a train ride to Rusape in order to cut my transport expenses. That friend of mine, Cordon, who had lent me some money, accompanied me to the train station in Harare. The trains were getting full during the day, so we went earlier in order to assure access to a ticket.

We had to devise a strategy for me to be able to get a place on the train that day. Cordon carried the satchel bag that had my things and the cigarettes which were lighter. I carried two crates of wine. Whilst I was struggling to deal with the pressure of the hundreds trying to clamber across me and through the very few entrances into this train to Mutare, it was easy for Cordon to enter because he had light luggage. When he had entered and found a place on this train that was not yet spilling with standing passengers, he called for me through the windows. I snuck those crates of wines through the window and followed through that same window.

The truck was already full. I was one of the lucky few forced to stand in the walkways of this truck. After bidding me farewell, Cordon disembarked from the train through the same window I had used to enter and left for home in Chitungwiza. Only one of my legs could really stand. There was no space. The other leg had to raise it a bit. There was nowhere else I could put it. The floors of this train were full of the passenger's luggage. That night, and to make my situation all the more problematic, the train inspectors allowed the train to fill to the brim. They said they didn't want to leave anyone outside that day. It became a hell of a situation for me. There were no spaces on the walkways to even stretch our bodies which were packed one against the other. So, my own silent journey started in these conditions.

The train rattled and clacked on its rails, eastbound. This train clanking seemed to repeat the question which had percolated to the surface of my mind: is-this-a-life, call-this-a-life, is-this-a-life...?

I only managed to access a seat at about three in the morning when some people disembarked at Nyazura town, some 40kms from Rusape town. I had been on the train from nine the previous night, standing on one leg at a time. From Nyazura, the train was traveling faster now, as if it were rushing to escape something. We arrived in Rusape early in the morning, at about four. I saw that morning sunrise arrive while still sitting on the railway platform.

At about eight that morning, I got a lift to Nyanga town. From there, I caught a bus ride to Nyamaropa. Before leaving, I had made arrangements with my other friend, Geoffrey, who had a rural home in Nyamaropa irrigation area to stay at his place with his younger brother, my namesake, a sister and a nephew who were staying there. Once there, I made some connections with a couple of boys who were friends of Geoffrey's young brother. The four of us, those two boys, Geoffrey's nephew and I, agreed to travel early morning the following day. The only reason Geoffrey's nephew decided to accompany me was to help to carry my things and to take care of me. He was a young boy, barely twelve years old. He and Geoffrey's little brother, who opted out of our journey, were still in early secondary school grades. But, while I was still new to this trade, the three of them were already masters.

"How long is the distance from here?" I asked those two boys. It was Monday, late afternoon. We were discussing the journey ahead while taking a bath in Kaerezi River. Kaerezi River was a immense, almost a lake on the move. We were bathing just off of a shallow crossing-point across the river. Having been around them before, I wasn't afraid of the crocs.

"I am not so sure. It's a mountainous walk so it's difficult to figure that out, but maybe 60 or 70km." One of those two boys, the one who seemed to be the leader of this pack, said.

I could only gape my mouth open, unbelieving what I was

hearing. I also thought to myself that those two little boys were trying to scare me, that our destination just couldn't really be that far.

"So, at what time are we leaving tomorrow?"

"We will come to pick you at your place at four in the morning. We have to clear the border areas before they start to patrol."

"When are the patrols enacted?"

"The soldiers are deployed at around six; so, we need those two hours to clear the border areas."

I nodded, knowing I could wake up at any time. I knew that wasn't a problem with me.

The problem was the government of Zimbabwe had started deploying soldiers on this border area to stem the tide of this illegal border crossing that had taken a huge swell of new members for some couple of months now. There was a gentlemen's agreement between Zimbabwe and Mozambique to allow both sets of people from these countries to cross once per week on separate days into each other's territories without passports so that they could buy the things they wanted. It now seemed that, on the Zimbabwean side, the trade had flourished into a bustling full scale market, which the Zimbabwean government, who could not collect taxes from it, said was illegal. The traders had devised the strategy to cross the borders early in the morning before the border patrol was enacted in order to avoid being captured and fined or jailed for illegally crossing this border.

The government in Zimbabwe found that it was difficult to man this border, though. There were many points to cross into Mozambique and the place was mountainous and thickly forested. On their part, the traders didn't think the government in Zimbabwe deserved any penny from these trade endeavors. To these struggling entrepreneurs, it was the same government that had destroyed their country and made them into ragged traders, market hawkers, and despondent unemployed vagrants. To these traders, this trek was a way in which they could keep afloat and feed their families. I fully subscribed to this view, as well. I didn't give a hoot about the corrupt government in Harare. All I wanted was to be able to live and provide for myself and my family.

At four in the morning on Tuesday, we were already crossing Kaerezi River, the border between the two countries. It was just a couple of hundreds of meters from Geoffrey's home. At about six, we were far into the mountains and bushes. Far into the unknown, I walked holding my head high, cracking the blue of the sky, chasing the pleated skirt of the Mozambican sun. It was hard going for me. I was trying to walk as fast as was possible to keep in touch with my young guides who were hardened walkers. They were good boys, though. When they saw I was far behind, they would wait for me so that I wouldn't get lost in those mountains.

The mountains and hills were covered thickly in vegetation, stabbed with sun shafts. Rock-bones jutted out here and there. As we trudged, the rivers sidled upon us unannounced. The lines of the mountains, forests, and rivers wound through this landscape. They would disappear for a time and then return, stoking me. I was carrying those two crates of wines and Geoffrey's nephew was carrying my bag with the cigarettes and other things. The other boys had lightweight luggage so I had to push myself just to keep pace with them. We walked fast and furious throughout the morning, and early afternoon.

It was just after midday when we took our first rest and ate our food. It was a mountainous area so it was difficult to walk for longer than we had done without resting, without taking liquids too. We drank water from a sweet stream near our resting place. The birds were exploding in the trees and some white pelicans' conversations, were a dirge of subjection, nearby.

"How long have we come on our journey?" I couldn't help asking them.

"We are almost halfway." The other one of those two little boys answered me this time.

"Halfway!" I couldn't believe we still had to walk more than we had already done that day.

"Yes." They chorused and I couldn't help grimacing.

"Are you tired?" He asked me innocently, but I knew he was sizzling with laughter inside.

"Tired, are you joking? I am sore all over my loins and feet."

They collapsed with laughter. I joined them, but couldn't see where the joke was. Maybe I was a complete joke to these little boys. I wanted to prove them wrong. They thought I was just a lazy city man; so, when we started on our journey again, I took the war to them and matched them. I was up to it and toughened for the rest of that journey.

The second half of the journey was even a lot more difficult for me than the first half because we were now climbing up the mountain ranges as the land rose. I could barely feel my feet. It was so hot with the stupor of the late afternoon heat. The heat soaking into me had an eerie quality of silence and reverie. We walked without rest and rested as we overlooked Nyadzonya camp on Nyadzonya Mountain. To the northwest of the mountain was a farm. The Nyadzonya camp was directly in front. I watched it; I stared at it. I tried to let its fortune soak into my future.

All that I had been waiting for was for a break, a chance to vault into a life, have a chance to fill it full of hits and misses. Instead, I felt like I was forever on the sidelines, waiting. We were talking, but I was watching the horizon below, intent on what we might find there.

Nyadzonya Mountain has very beautiful stones. I thought I saw gold, but couldn't have taken it. Besides being too heavy to carry, I was afraid of getting lost in this mountain by falling too far behind my guides. It is a sacred mountain I was told later. So it might have been a sacrilege to take its gold away. They said that the mountain is full of secrets. Maybe, there was something there which the mountain refused to share with me, a hidden fortune which waits for those who know its design and whisperings.

Unfortunately, I was not that person. I was just trying to keep my feet under me. Going down this mountain offered a different challenge. It was so steep. I could barely control myself from tumbling down on my face. We were basically trotting, going down this mountain, slipping and sliding the whole way down. When we got to the foot of the mountain, we simply collapsed. There, we took some time to stretch our legs and massage our feet and calves.

That evening, we arrived at Nyadzonya, the place where some thousands of thousands of my countrymen died in the liberation war from Ian Smith's bombs. As the sun sat on its iridescent throne on top on Nyadzonya Mountain, I remembered the stories I had read of this place and the liberation war in the novel, "A Silent Journey from the East" by Isheunese Valentine Mazorodze. The book spoke of how the many regular people made their journeys from different parts of Zimbabwe to Mozambique as they joined the liberation war. Then, the newly trained warriors returned into Zimbabwe as liberation war fighters.

I remembered the stories of how Nyathi, a liberation war soldier who had sold out, directed Smith's soldiers and pilots to Nyadzonya camp which they bombed to the ground, bloodying the landscape and the river. The galling thing was to realize that these liberation warriors were the now the same people who were in the government in Harare. The people who had liberated the country had also mismanaged it to the ground. They are all like Nyathi to me.

Now, I had made the same journey. The thought occurred to me that I was here trying to liberate myself, though as another kind of warrior with a much different ideology. I was not angry. Time cures all wounds, I thought. I didn't want to create any pain or strife. I simply had to liberate myself from the kind of life those who had liberated us had now developed as the model for our nation. I needed food; I needed shelter; I needed a future. There was no doubt about it; this was a liberation war I was now fighting for myself and my family.

When I heard of the place and read stories about it, I thought of it as a well established town. What I saw that day shocked me. The first thing that hit me, in fact it bowled me over, was the smell of dirt, of shit. It smelled of sewage all over the place. The river that runs through the middle of this place was even full of shit. I remember from my history lessons that it was the same river that had turned red from the blood of the people who were killed during the liberation war, when the waters in the river had carried the lives and hopes of so many of my countrymen with it downstream so many years before. Now, it was some greenish brown sewage color. I reflected a moment on how this river was a mirror, reflecting the reality of a whole nation for anyone astute enough to look.

When walking through the walkways, not roads because there are no roads at this place, I had to carefully watch my step, to keep my foot from stepping onto the shit that covered everything in this place. Except for the camp commemorating where the liberators were housed which featured modern buildings, the rest of the place was made up of small huts of dagga and poles, roofed with plastics or grass. Unfortunately, it didn't take us too longer before we realized there was not much trade happening at that place for the things we had just carried across the mountains.

We didn't stay longer so we disbanded that place for a much better and bigger town, Villa de Katandike to the south along the Tete highway. A couple of hours later, we took a truck ride to Katandike. We did not see much that night, but we found some place to sleep at the market area of that town, a dilapidated hall which was bare, dusty and dirty with sewage flowing across the entrance to the place. The doors were old, chipped, and decaying.

In the morning, we discovered the town of Katandike. It was just as dirty and smelling of shit as Nyadzonya. Luckily, our trade went much smoother here. I couldn't make a profit, though neither did I sell my wares at a loss. I took whatever best offer I could get because I knew I couldn't have stayed another day there.

Without wasting another moment in that shit-stained end of the world outpost, we started on our journey back home. We agreed we weren't going to be able to take a lift back. While there were some trucks plying this route to about halfway of our journey, we wanted to save whatever money we had, so we decided to walk again. In the middle of our climb up the mountain overlooking Katandike, I was so tired such that I couldn't raise my legs anymore. Fatigue simply had rounded my shoulders. I couldn't take it anymore. It was so hot and my head was beginning to show a tremor of some sort, banging hard and painfully. My chest was exploding so I told the boys to continue with the journey, that I was taking a rest. I would take a lift to catch up with them. After a bit of some deliberation, they left me. I wasn't afraid of getting lost anymore; in fact, I was past caring about my life.

I rested a bit and then walked a bit up the mountain road. It meandered up the mountain as if it was trying to find the best way up through the mountain, almost like an extension of my now melancholic personality. For nearly an hour, no truck came through, so I continued with my slow journey at my own pace. Later, when a truck did come through, I could see that it was packed full already. I knew she would simply pass me if I didn't do something drastic to stop her. So, I stood in the middle of the road and waved, gesticulating like a policeman patrolling the road, for her to stop the truck and pick me up.

She stopped at the last moment, at my feet, almost running me down. I hadn't budged a foot. I didn't give a damn anymore. What's not to die about my situation? I thought.

She shouted some angry expletives at me, but I kept cool. I apologized and begged her to pick me up. She said her truck was full, but I countered that I could squeeze in. We argued for long minutes until she budged. I thanked her and squeezed in. It didn't matter that I was almost hanging off the outer boards of the load body of the truck; I was still glad to be on my way home.

She told me that she was going to her farm on top of the

mountains. She later told me that she was a former Zimbabwean white commercial farmer who had relocated to Mozambique after being displaced in the farm invasions. Her farm had been in the Macheke area, another rich soils farming area like Mushazhike.

Her new farm was beside the road and half the distance to where the trucks would usually end. I was just happy to be off my feet for a moment. She told us about the many farmers from Macheke region who had disbanded to Mozambique as we helped her load the sheep in the truck's load body which she said she was taking back to Katandike for slaughter. She told us she had a butcher shop at Katandike, as well as a super market.

After helping her, I started on my own journey. I knew my colleagues were still behind me in the mountains so it was easy to walk slowly, at my own pace. I knew that when they caught up with me, I would have covered a bit of distance. I couldn't get lost this time because I simply had to follow the road and the road had a lot of Zimbabweans on their way home. So long as I couldn't get lost, I had no fear. I even met up with some old friend on his way to Katandike. We did catch up near a stream as we rested.

It was there, by the stream, where my colleagues caught up with me. From there onwards, I tried to keep pace with them, but it was still too much for me. As we reached the middle of the journey, where the trucks ended, it was getting darker so the boys increased pace. I told them I couldn't keep pace. I was simply dead in all my limbs, even inside me. I told them to leave me and that I wanted to rest. I had given up; there was nothing left in me.

This time they debated for such a long time. Geoffrey's nephew said that they couldn't leave me behind anymore because it was dark. The two other boys said they had to keep walking fast so that they could reach home quickly. They were afraid of something. In fact, they were almost frozen with fear. I felt the fear and heard it in their breath. I didn't know what they were afraid of. Even Geoffrey's nephew was scared, but he couldn't leave me in that middle of nowhere at night.

So, he told them to go and that he would stay with me. That little boy knew it was dangerous to leave me alone in the middle of this forest. I didn't know at the time that the forest has dangerous lions to deal with on top of hyenas, wolves and leopards. He told me about this later, the next day, when I asked him why he hadn't left me and what the other boys were so afraid of the previous night.

That night, we continued on our journey at my pace. It was now night so it got cooler and cooler. I could walk longer distances before I got tired, stumbling leg-blind, eyes-blind, even knowledge-blind in the dimness of the night. In the darkness, though, we got lost several times in those mountains. I could hear the wind in the grass and far away sounds that cut the night like a thin, sharp knife.

We made it across Kaerezi River a kilometer from the place we should have crossed it. We crossed it unharmed. In me, there was only a sense of something, or of someone who had tried so many times and failed and now finally had given up hope. I had a feeling of profound abandonment over my soul, a crushing feeling. We reached his home at two in the morning on Thursday. We ate and I slept in the kitchen. I couldn't even make the journey to the bedroom which was just about 5 meters from the kitchen. I just collapsed after eating and slept.

I felt like I was in hell and someone was raking the coals. I just felt my life lifting at its edges. I think I was on the brink of a profound exhaustion. I didn't die, even though some might say it really happened anyway. I woke up in the morning and made the journey to the bedroom and fell back into a stupor, sleeping through that morning. I ate in the afternoon and returned back to sleep, woke up in the evening, ate and returned back to sleep. I slipped in and out of consciousness throughout that day; my body numbed from the enormous exertion of the previous day.

The following morning, I could feel some sense in my feet and body, but I was so wasted from the diarrhea that I had had for a couple of days and from the walking. All my clothes didn't fit me anymore. I had to tighten the belt a little bit to make my trousers fit me. On that Friday midmorning, I took a lift back to Chitungwiza. I went home. I tried to laugh. I laughed. I tried to forget. Maybe, I even did forget a little. But everyone reminded me of this: everyone who saw me the following weeks thought I had been ill or down with something. They couldn't understand how I had lost so much weight in less than a week.

More than a few pounds, what I knew I had lost with that journey was the will to fight anymore. My mind, body, and spirit, the triangle of life had been broken. I just didn't give a damn about my life anymore. For weeks afterwards, I just folded my arms and waited for whatever life would throw at me. I just didn't care. I just couldn't go for anything anymore. I had lost the passion for life.

I was dead inside.

Chapter 9: Mr. ZINYAMA

I hadn't seen him for over two weeks. It was at the height of the June campaigns, days of the run-off. For some time, I couldn't ask his wife where he was. He lived a couple of blocks from our home. We had often talked through the two yard fences that separated us. I thought maybe that he had taken an international trip for he was a truck driver. He sometimes would travel to surrounding countries, transporting different kinds of stuff. It would be after some couple or so weeks before I would see him again. When I saw him, I was shocked. He could barely walk. At first, I thought he was ill so I asked him.

"What's the matter with you, Mr. Zinyama, were you ill?

"No." He looked at me funny, sort of sideways, and then said, "You don't know, do you?"

"No, I don't know anything. What's the matter? You can barely stand on your bones let alone walk. What happened?"

"I was beaten up."

"Beaten up, but who beat you? We never heard anything this side." I was thinking maybe he was beaten up at his home by the ZANUPF youths and national youth service members, the notorious Green Bombers, who had become at this time so rowdy and dangerous that they had beaten some people around Zengeza Township. The youths had a political base at the fringes of our street. They were becoming a real cause of concern to us.

Yesterday, I had heard them harassing my next door neighbor. I had to watch helplessly as they took her two sugar bags, each with 10*2kgs bags of sugar which my neighbor was selling at the open market, earning a bit to get by. The times were so hard on everyone and losing that kind of stuff was a hard thing for her. There was nothing we could do or say about it. There were over twenty young people wielding an assortment of weaponry. We had to take it quietly as they grabbed all the stuff for their own consumption purposes at their base. It was even galling and shameful to hear the leader of this group, a local girl, rationalizing that taking what didn't belong to them was the only way they could take care of themselves.

They also knew they could as well do as they wished because there was no recourse to the law for everyone else. The country was being ruled by warlords and these youths were the political strong-arms of these scoundrels' power. The police were now silent spectators, if not also instigating participants.

This was what I first thought had happened to Mr. Zinyama. My hypothesis was almost correct; though, the truth was typical of the times: a lot more disturbing and painful. It showed me how pain could sound at its first ugly utterance, its dark presence being conjured into the world by simple words.

"A week ago, I went to our rural home in Rukweza, Rusape, in the Nyazura area. Do you know the place, John?"

"Yes, I know the place. My mother comes from that area."

"Is it?"

"Yep, in Handina village, I have been there a couple of times."

"So, when I was coming back, I decided to take back with me 10 bags of maize grains for consumption here as you can see there is no maize meal flour in the shops. I thought it could push us for some months."

"Definitely, it would, for sure." I agreed with him. Maize was now a rare commodity and had become expensive, yet it was the staple diet of the whole country.

"So, I loaded the bags on the carrier of a bus that was on its way this side. On the way, just after turn-off to the headlands by Rusape on the Mutare road, our bus was stopped by the ZANUPF youths, a number of army and police people, and the Green Bombers."

I could only say, "Hey."

I knew that it meant trouble to be stopped by those bloody Green Bombers. They were now an awful lot. No one could find patterns to their mayhem.

"They demanded to search the bus, of course. They took everything they could lay hands on which even included money. If they found you with anything they wanted, they would find a reason to take it from you. If you complain, then they would tell you to wait on the side, outside the bus. I made the mistake of trying to reason with them so that they would take maybe half of my consignment of maize, but they started shouting at me telling me that I was one of those people who were fuelling the black market in Harare by hoarding maize. They told me to wait by the side, outside the bus, if I wanted my maize back."

I shook my head, guessing where this story was going.

He picked right up and kept on with his narrative, "After they had taken their loot of everything they wanted, they let the driver proceed with the journey to Harare without me and the other four guys who had also protested against this confiscation. They took us to the base. It was late evening by the time we arrived at their base which was deep in the farming area of the headlands. I was still hemming and hawing all the way to the base, but they just ignored me all along to this place. When we arrived at the base, they cooked their own food, ate and divided some of the things they had confiscated with the exception of the food items. They pooled the food items together including my 10 bags of maize grains as a food reserve bank."

He shook his head at me before continuing, "They didn't give me any food, but gave the other four guys food saying that they had not been the nuisance that I was. They said they were punishing me for protesting too much. At about nine that night, they went to the base which was just some few meters from their own tents for the night's pungwe (the night vigil). They forcefully took us there too. The leader of the band told us that they wanted to make a good example of me. He commanded the other four guys to hold me. They were told to bring me to the middle. He then told them to lift me to about waist level. They held me suspended in air, stretched." He stretched out his arms and legs to show me an approximation of how he had been restrained.

Then, he continued, "He commanded the base brigands of the Green Bombers and ZANUPF youths to start singing revolutionary songs. So a songfest of ongoing celebration erupted, singing as if singing for the one no longer seen. They started singing map songs, compass songs, village songs, signal songs. They sung sorrowful songs laced with the joy of their faces as they danced around me, clapping hands, whistling, being heartfelt. They never left, of the songs they sung, a single lyric unsung. The leader stood there throughout, watching me. Then, he took off his belt and started beating me by my buttocks, underneath my feet whilst they were dancing, singing and circling me, beating their drums."

There was no exhilaration in his voice as he spoke of these

rousing songs sung to him on that fateful night.

"I was being blasted underfoot, on my buttocks, with his painful belt, leaving lobes of blood where the belt kneaded into my flesh. That belt tore my flesh, as a prodding inquisition, the fraying, the fletching, the shelling of my skin, and the haunting drums. When he was tired, he gave the belt to the next person. I was beaten for nearly an hour without a break. Even though I was no longer howling with pain, they didn't stop."

I saw the helpless pain flash across my dear neighbor's face.

"They stopped for some 10 minutes or so. They also commanded those four guys to rest as well. Those four guys just about dumped me and forgot about me as they rested, talked, and laughed between themselves, in spasms of neutral laughter in the afterglow of the fire. After ten minutes, they started beating me again. It stretched for long minutes. I was drifting back and forth from consciousness.

Then, in one fell swoop, I passed out. It must have been a flurry of a eating. I don't remember what happened afterwards. When I woke up the following morning, I was in Rusape General Hospital. The blisters on my buttocks and underfoot throbbed like a heartbeat."

"Who took you there?"

I couldn't believe what I was hearing. Of course, I had heard of this kind of situation before, but not so close to home. It was the same type of punishment meted out to my church auntie's relative in the Mutoko area, in another province. I never thought I would really come across someone I knew who went through the same kind of thing. It was a hard kind of listening, subjecting myself to someone else's textures and rhythms, trying to give them my own words and meanings.

"The nurses later told me that some well-wisher brought me to the hospital after finding me dumped by the Mutare road."

"Hey that's so terrible. I am so sorry." That's all that I could manage to say to him. I also told him of my auntie's relative, of the same predicament that she went through as well. He replied and concurred with my observation that he was lucky to be alive.

"That's what makes me so grateful, to be alive. Not only that, John." His reply was darker, and nearer to the earth than air.

"Not only that, but what else, Mr. Zinyama?"

"When I came to in the hospital, the ward I was in was packed full with people nursing different kinds of injuries. Some had hands chopped off, John, some had ears lopped off, eyes gorged, even feet which had been hacked off. The mutilation matched the intensity of the militias' hatred. I felt lucky that none of my limbs had been chopped off. The hospital was so crowded, John, by people who were made into cripples by the Green Bombers and ZANUPF youths in the Rusape area. Once I was conscious, they released me since I was fine and could recover at home. They said they wanted to make space for some more victims who were coming from the killing fields of Rusape. I came home a week ago with nothing. I couldn't stand on my feet or sit on my haunches, John. All this week, I have been inside."

"It's so sad. So, how are you feeling now, Mr. Zinyama?" I couldn't also help asking myself what would feel human at that depth.

"I am a bit better now, John. At least I can stand on my legs." He said that in a voice like the trim, measured lines of an epauleted form; the sadness welled in his eyes, boiling as if they had peered unblinkingly for the last hour.

"I am so sorry, Mr. Zinyama."

"It's alright now. It was so terrible, but I am happy I am still alive, you know?"

Chapter 10: MBUYA CHITUNGWIZA

For as long as I remember, we called her Mbuya Chitungwiza, that is our way of calling her Grandmother Chitungwiza, a respectful nickname earned because she was so much a part of our community's identity. I remember when we were little boys calling her Mbuya Chitungwiza. She was well known in Chitungwiza, both by the politicians and the general populace of this city.

Chitungwiza is a populous dormitory slum city to the south of Harare. This is where we lived. It is a city of poor people and workers; it fed Harare with cheap labour. She used to brag that even the president knew her for she was such an avid grassroots activist of the ZANUPF party. She was also a traditional dancer. She used to get invited to all traditional dance ceremonies in and around Chitungwiza and Harare. Every little kid in this city knew her. We were neighbours and we even became known by the general Chitungwiza populace as Mbuya Chitungwiza's nephews and nieces.

We were not related to her in any way, though. We were just neighbours with her. On a personal level and for many years, we have always been very close. She was my grandmother, not a blood one, but one connected with me emotionally. Her presence in my life was wonderful, at least most of the time.

We disagreed on only one issue: ZANUPF. She was a blind ZANUPF supporter. She also thought everyone should feel the same way about ZANUPF, especially those who were close to her. She used to use fear of retribution to force her blood daughter and nephews and nieces, and even their children to join and participate in ZANUPF activities. She tried to do the same with me several times, but I wouldn't budge. I hated ZANUPF with a passion. There were arguments, fierce arguments across the wire fence that separated our two residences. Just seeing her wearing ZANUPF's regalia, especially a Zambia cloth with Mugabe's image got me going. I would provoke her and say angry things.

"How is Mugabe's wife today? I can see he looks so happy to be there with his face on your buttocks."

I always said that in greeting her. I always called her Mugabe's wife. A lot of people called women this upon learning of their support of Mugabe and the ZANUPF. It was no secret that Mugabe's powers came from the women's league members; a group of women who were ZANUPF members, a group Mbuya Chitungwiza was a member of. She always bristled, even when she knew quite well that I was simply provoking her.

"Yes, I am Mugabe's wife. It's gotten me a lot of things like this Zambia cloth. I got my house from supporting Mugabe, you know that?"

Of course, she was telling lies about the house. These slums were built by the Rhodesians long before Mugabe came to power. I reminded her of this sometimes; other times, I just let that pass. It was her point of strength in these arguments for or against Mugabe. She always said that she even got the kitchen things from Mugabe himself. There was this legend that Mugabe himself had come to her homestead and donated furniture for an entire home. I knew I couldn't fight her on that.

When it supposedly happened, we were still young and living at our rural home, so we hadn't seen anything firsthand. We couldn't dispute this. It seemed I couldn't really fight her on anything, those days. In her mind, she was so set on her belief that the ZANUPF was the only party that should rule the country. It was Mugabe's belief, so it became ZANUPF's belief, as well. Mugabe believed that he had to rule the country for life, and that ZANUPF had to rule until the horses grow horns. It was even becoming obvious that if you criticize her about ZANUPF, she would relapse into blind support of the party and start criticizing the MDC, an opposition party in Zimbabwe.

Mbuya Chitungwiza also thought everyone who was against ZANUPF was a member of the MDC. Not that she was far from the truth, the real issue here, though, was that the ZANUPF had destroyed the country through their stupid policies over the twenty eight years the party had been in power. Since it was election time, it was easy to let her know about that and to help her in getting worked up about the issue. I always found some opportunity to remind her of her party's failures and empty promises.

"Mbuya, why do you still blindly support a party that has made us beggars in our own country?"

"...Because it won us the independence, Muzukuru. Nephew, MDC, the party that you support is a stooge for the white imperialists and colonizers who are trying to take the country back through this MDC."

She would hit back that way. The funny thing was she was even sounding a lot more like Mugabe those days. That was the type of vitriolic rhetoric coming from Mugabe's mouth those days. Mbuya Chitungwiza had come into the city a couple of days before. We were a just a day away from the election.

She had been staying at her small farm plot that she had

squatted on illegally in the Beatrice area. The government helped them to forcefully displace white commercial farmers from their lands and took those farms. A few of the large farms were divided into small plots and taken up by the likes of Mbuya Chitungwiza who never in their entire lives had been farmers.

The bulk of those farms were parceled to Mugabe's cronies in the ZANUPF party. It had been a chaotic and destructive land reform program. It had resulted in a chaotic situation for Zimbabwe. The country that used to feed the whole southern African region couldn't feed itself anymore. It was now an empty basket case. I reminded her of that.

"You know, Mbuya, it is better to support the MDC, at least they didn't steal anyone's farms and mismanage them to the ground."

"At least, ZANUPF gave us the farms. We now have places of our own where we will be buried, on our own farms, you see!"

"So, you mean you are so happy that ZANUPF has afforded you more land to bury yourselves in after dying from the hunger it has created. Do you mean that, Mbuya?"

"Nobody is dying from hunger." She bristled. Such was her mind-bending faith in the ZANUPF.

"People are dying all over the country from hunger. ZANUPF never would admit to that, you know that, Mbuya."

"It is because there is no one dying. We never heard that on the radio."

"You mean on ZANUPF radio stations; yet, people are dying, Mbuya."

"Do you mean MDC people? We don't give a damn about MDC people. They should get their food from the western countries that they are friends with."

"I don't care whether the people dying are ZANUPF or MDC. People are dying and it's because of these ZANUPF policies. Mbuya, 'to weld nothing other than a stance is to let the river reverse its flow,' you should know that yourself."

"Nobody is dying, Muzukuru." She declared. I wasn't even sure she heard me or even smelled anything of what I was saying.

We would fight around this sometimes, but to no avail. It was becoming a tiresome exercise because it never changed her mind set. There has never been anything as forlorn and as sad as an opinion. She would go down fighting for ZANUPF. Some three months later, we would have the same argument again. This time, she had returned for the run-off election in June. It galled me that she could even waste her precious time to come all the way from Beatrice which is nearly 60 km from Chitungwiza just for those dead ball elections.

No sane person was still interested in those elections anymore. The MDC had withdrawn from those elections, but Mugabe was going ahead in a sick one-man show. He wanted to win an election against no one really. Mbuya Chitungwiza had come all the way to vote and participate in this dead election.

I later got my revenge a couple of days after this farce of an election which, of course Mugabe won with almost 100% of the vote. She came to me in the morning asking for some bus fare money back to Beatrice. Even though I still loved her, I told her straight away that I wasn't going to waste the little hard-earned money that I had for this excursion, no. I wasn't going to support her with transport monies for her to come all the way and support ZANUPF through a vote that I had financed in any way. I told her if she wanted travel fares she had to go and ask for such monies from the ZANUPF, whom she still blindly supported. I told her that she would just as well walk back to her farm, that I didn't give a damn. I even suggested sarcastically that she could get the monies from her daughter who was listening to us.

"But, don't you see: she has nothing herself. Her job doesn't earn her much. You know that, Muzukuru. She also has a big family she is looking after."

That daughter also bristled with anger over my sarcasm. She scolded me for being uppity and proud, for thinking that I now had a lot of money and for refusing to help an old lady. I replied to her obstinately.

"No, I won't help her to continue destroying our lives, no. She is the reason why you are even struggling to take care of your own family, her nieces and nephews at that! No, I am not going to feel sorry for her this time. No sense of guilt will change me this time around."

"But, she is an old harmless lady."

Edge to centre, so the world had to go out of its way for her again!

"Yes. I am an old lady, Muzukuru. I am over 80 years old and it's not easy for us to take to new ideas. MDC is for you, young people. Not for us, old people."

I could have told her that there were old people in the MDC, but I felt drained. I only said one word.

"Whatever!"

I seemed able to express only that word, but it felt more liberating than restrictive. Then, I stormed back into the house and left mother and daughter shocked and aghast at my behavior. I didn't give a damn anymore. I was so bitter in those days. I didn't even know what would become of my life.

Chapter 11: A LOOK IN THE MIRROR

Before the prevalence of the mirror as a common household item, and in a rather backward village of Ruchera, in the eastern highlands of Zimbabwe, there lived a boy and a girl. His name was Chakupa. Chakupa was in love with the beautiful Runako.

It all happened when Runako's uncle on her mother's side came for a visit and brought her a present. It was wrapped in covers. In order to enjoy her gift alone, she took it outside. As she removed the wrappers, there was a small hand mirror. When she looked into the mirror, she saw a very beautiful girl. In awe and wonder she joyously rushed to find her lover who was alone at his parents' homesteads and said.

"Chakupa, I want to show you the wonderful gift that my uncle gave me."

"What gift?" Chakupa asked.

"This one..." She said, showing him.

"In the gift, there is a very beautiful young lady."

"You must be very stupid, Runako. How can a person fit into that object?" Chakupa quipped.

Yet, for all his knowing that no person could fit into the object, he proved himself as stupid as Runako when he looked into the mirror.

"But, I am seeing a rather dirty ugly man." He differed.

Upon which a long endless augment ensued, Runako insisted that there was a very beautiful young lady while Chakupa adamantly said that there was an ugly boy. So they agreed to enlist the help of knowledgeable elders. They went to Chakupa's grandfather who was considered the wisest elder of the entire village. Upon arrival Runako and Chakupa let in the old man into their object of contention.

Sekuru, a very calm and wise man, in order to prove these young stupid adults were wrong, asked them to have a look into the object of their augment, upon which was given the mirror.

"Oh! My God in heaven!"

He jumped fearfully when he peeped into the mirror because he was afraid of being killed by the rather wild angry animal that he just saw.

"You are so stupid. There is a very wild, angry and ready to attack old baboon."

He looked at those two young adults while exuding visionary and untouchable ray of the sages' wisdom in his bearing and said, "If I were you, then I would stop looking into that very dangerous object, unless, of course, if you are tired of your lives."

Upon which another augment ensued.

Chapter 12: THE DARK HAIRED GIRL

We were out in Harare. It was the end of March, a Wednesday, I had given notice at my workplace. I had decided to leave the country for South Africa. Going to work now was a wasteful exercise. The wages I was getting at the end of the month weren't even enough to get me through the first week after payday. Necessities were beyond my reach, and the truth was: even if I could have afforded to buy some of the things, the things I needed and wanted were not even available in the stores anyway. Business at the company where I worked, a motor vehicle sales company, was down. We were spending days on end without any sale. I was spending most of those days getting into queues to procure basic necessities like bread, mealy-meal, sugar and other commodities.

Times when I was at work, I was busy looking for employment outside the country. Lately I had been concentrating on South Africa. I had given up on getting better work in Zimbabwe. Since I was seeing through my last month of the three months notice, I wasn't so keen on working anymore. There were other things holding more of my attention at the time. Natasha, my girlfriend for slightly more than four months, was enjoying much of my time.

Our relationship was one of those drifting things, but we were spending a lot of time together. I knew she liked me a lot but I wasn't so sure of how I felt for her. That day, I was looking for job offers in South Africa. The jobs that I could qualify for had a lot of other demands that I couldn't meet like a work permit, international driver's license, etc. I didn't have the money to access these extra qualifications or trainings; I had been saving for a year now and it was just enough to get me transport to South Africa.

All I had been able to afford was an emergency travel document which was cheaper and less difficult to access than a passport. I had no one in South Africa. I had no other arrangements with anyone in South Africa so I didn't know where I was going to be staying as I would be looking around for work. I had just a bit of change money for food for a few days.

I got bored with the results I was getting from the job bank I was using so I decide I needed a break. I called Natasha.

"Hello, Tasha...hi, baby!" I said after she had received my call. She was so happy, from the tone of her voice, to be hearing from me.

"Hi Tendai, how is your day today?"

"Boring!"

"Are you bored? What's boring you?" She asked me.

"Work I suppose. I think it's about everything...do you think you could come over here Tasha? We could hang out, sort of. I want to talk to you about something else." Natasha wasn't going to work anymore those days. She had been offloaded at her workplace, at some fast food place in Harare city centre so I knew such a kind of offer was one she couldn't have refused.

"Tendai, you want me to come there right now, now? Are you not working today?"

"There is not much work to do today."

"But, I don't have the fares into town."

"Can you go to my place, Tasha? I am talking to my cousin now. Get the bus fares from George and come over here. I will give you the return fares when we meet."

"Ok, I will do that."

"Cool..."

"Love you, Tendai."

"Love you too, Tasha."

I hung up and phoned my cousin and asked him to lend Natasha some money for her transport into town. George was still working at a company in the outskirts of Harare, the other side of that city. For him to get to work he had to take two lifts to work, so he had been only going to work once or twice per week. He had just about given up like me. He didn't care whether he got fired at his job or not. He reasoned the best thing was to stay home most days than to waste the little he had by going to work. There was not that much work at his place.

She came into town and then phoned me when she had disembarked at the bus stop in Harare city centre at about twelve noon. I lied to my immediate boss that I was off to do car valuations at Kingdom bank. It was easy to dupe him because I had been carrying out vehicle valuations at this company that week. I was happy to see her waiting for me at the bus stop. I hugged her feelingly, kissed her to let her know that I was really enjoying seeing her. She had let her hair go back to a soft medium natural black. Her breasts and buttocks were big and jutted out proudly. She was an attractive girl by any stretch.

I took her to the Chicken Inn at the corner of Inez Terrence and George Silundika Street. It was the biggest there was in the city so I knew we would definitely find the food we were looking for. She ordered a quarter chicken and chips. I did the same. Though it was expensive, I didn't mind wasting a bit of the money on these orders. I was past caring about a lot of things. I also thought it was a good and fitting goodbye for Natasha. I just wanted to spoil her a bit.

And so, we talked silly-nothings whilst we worked on the chicken and chips. After that, we ordered ice cream for dessert. We nibbled our ice cream cones as we loitered through the dense afternoon crowds of the city. She said we could go to Harare gardens where we could sit and talk, so we made our way to the northerly direction towards these gardens. When we had found a good spot to sit in the gardens, I told her straight away that I would be leaving the country for South Africa.

"South Africa, but why, Tendai?"

"I have been serving notice at my workplace, Natasha, for almost three months now. This is my last month. I would really like to try to get a job down in South Africa. There is not much work at the company where I am working right now, so it's a matter of time before I am laid off. Instead of waiting, I'd like to take the initiative now. There are bound to be better prospects in South Africa, I should think?"

"But, you never told me that's what you have been planning to do all these months, why Tendai?"

"We have just only lately started getting serious, Tasha. I wanted to tell you; I have been meaning to do that, but..."

"So, where does that leave us, Tendai?"

"I love you, Natasha. I would like you to eventually join me." She loved me anyway and I knew it. It's so calming to know someone loves you. Confidences in another's love can still our own thoughts almost to a halt.

"When?"

"I am not so sure, yet."

She started sniffling and I knew she was crying, head bent in supplication. She somehow knew that, if I left, then it might be difficult for me to return back, let alone to let her join me there. I asked her why she was crying. She said nothing. I asked her if she was crying because she thought I wouldn't be returning back. She asked me if I would really return back. I told her that I would be returning back in about three month's time, a job or no job. She didn't want me to go. She said I could get a job, another job at another company in Zimbabwe, so I should stay. I told her I could get a better job in South Africa and that it would only be for a couple or so months that we would be separated. I couldn't have told her I was going for the long haul. I still wanted to hold onto her. I didn't want to hurt her unnecessarily. That afternoon, I had to spend the time trying to convince her that it was a good move for the two of us in the long run and that she had to have hope in us. I was selling a hope that I didn't have, but I couldn't have told her that. Instead, I told her that we would, eventually, be together.

That afternoon, I did not return back to my workplace. I phoned Mr. Rusere, my boss and told him that the work I was doing would see me through that afternoon and that I wouldn't be returning back to the offices after I was through. I told him that I would go home straight away upon completing my last assignment. Mr Rusere was a good manager. For the three years, we had been working together and he had never made any unnecessary fuss over anything unless it was absolutely necessary to do so. I knew he would never check my story. He said it was ok with him. That afternoon, we loitered through the streets. As we strolled through the streets, I talked her into the vision that I had for the two of us, making her feel like a part of the deal. Earlier, we had argued, but we had gotten past it and were getting along fine. Yet, I knew there was still a question she hadn't asked me, or maybe she was hesitating to ask me.

Later, we returned home together. We were at her parents' place where she stayed with her parents. We were at the gates and I was saying goodbye to her when she asked me why I was saying goodbye to her as if I was leaving for South Africa right away. For all those months we had been seeing one another, I had never said goodbye to her when leaving her for the day. We would just hug and kiss when it was time to leave each other's company, so I answered her honestly.

"I told you, Tasha. I will be leaving for South Africa." I couldn't help reminding her.

"Are you going like right now, like tomorrow, Tendai?"

"Yes, I am leaving tomorrow, Tasha. I thought you realised that?"

"You are joking...are you joking, Tendai?" Sadness and pain coming to squat on top of those words, she said. "What's the matter with you, Tendai?" She said that in a sheepish voice, like a little girl.

"There is nothing the matter, Tasha. And, no, I am not joking. I have already prepared for an afternoon departure, tomorrow afternoon, Tasha."

"But, why the rush, Tendai?"

I knew it simply would have to be performance art from there onwards; some part of my heart told me I had never really been in it with her.

"I am not rushing anything, Tasha. I have already made the

arrangements. I don't see why I should stay around any longer. If I go early, Natasha, then I will be able to return sooner. I also want to go before they are many complications with my travel arrangements at the border."

"How are you traveling to South Africa?"

"I will be jumping the border through Limpopo River. A lot of people are doing that these days. I don't have enough money to apply for a Visa now."

"Limpopo River is infested with crocodiles, Tendai. Are you crazy? Are you not afraid of the crocodiles? Why are you risking your life like that....?" She couldn't complete the sentence because she was crying again. Drowning in the river and getting feasted upon was a painful and frightening thing for her to bear as was life to innocent children born in harm's way. A man's life is difficult, for how is he supposed to provide for his family? Isn't it in our own undoing that new possibilities arise? I had to go through the motions again, trying to convince her that I will be okay and that no danger would befall me.

By the time I left her for home, I knew somehow Natasha had come to accept the inevitability of our separation. There was no need to explain to her that the chain was now broken and that the curve of the horizon would be my guide. She was still despondent, but tried to smile up a bit and be polite. When I left her, she was still sneezing silently. I couldn't even ask her to accompany me to Mbudzi turn-off on the outskirts of the south western suburbs of Harare where I was going to take a truck to South Africa on the morrow. Trucks were cheaper, so I would save a bit. Plus, the truck driver agreed to link me with the Malaitshas (border gangsters) who were doing some roaring trade helping people cross into South

Africa through Limpopo River.

The morrow morning, I was surprised when she came over to accompany me to Mbudzi turn off. She was wearing her best dress with tiny flowers all over it, with black buttons from above her naval up to her neck. I couldn't help staring at the buttons; buttons have always fascinated me. It's exciting to know that, when watching both the insides and the outsides of a girl, buttons are the threshold. But, that day, I didn't like seeing her. I just wanted to go without a fuss that day. I just felt like I could sort of take-off, give a spark of flight, a light departure for a moribund heart.

Maybe, she perceived my rawness; she didn't make any fuss over me. She was meek, afraid I was going to ream her for being late. We didn't talk that much as I made my final preparations, even as she accompanied me. She seemed much calmer, not exactly grounded though, hiding behind politeness like a shell and choosing to nurse her grief alone.

We took some chicken bus to Mbare Musika (Mbare market place) in Harare. On our way, we were basically quiet, estranged. Her facial muscles were not moving much, her posture was extremely drowsy, shoulders folding inside. Her chest hiding inside those shoulders, she was troubled. Keeping to the surface, I did not dare invade her chosen cell. I had nothing more to say to her, nothing to promise her. So, I was watching the sides of the road which were green with brush. The tall grass sighed, hanging suspended in the day's clear air. Here a chinaberry tree, and there a mimosa tree, I watched the acacia trees, poplar tree, and, in them, the bluebells reeling. They danced in the air without paying our heaviness any mind.

When we cleared Irvine farm and were hugging the outskirts of the Waterfall suburb, we started walking to the bus's doors. I had very little on me, just a satchel with a clean pair of clothes, some food, some toiletries, emergency travel documents and some money. I knew we would be walking quite a lot for part of our journey so I travelled light. We disembarked before the bus entered the circle and turned off to Mbare Musika. The southerly breeze was blowing slowly and the late morning shadows were rubbing across the ground.

There were a lot of trucks coming through, resting and refueling on their way to South Africa, so I didn't have to wait and hang around longer. I did let a couple of those trucks pass and boarded the third one that came through. I hugged her goodbye; I kissed her in a way that I didn't think I could do. I told her again that we will be together again soon, that I loved her. Despite my conflicted heart, I wasn't playing. I really wanted to take credit for those small three words and be less lonely. Closing her eyes, she linked her hands to mine and started pulling me in; hoping for the best. I felt her smile all around me. I would really love to have juggled the stars for her, but I also wanted to love her in a way that would leave me free.

I left her and boarded the truck destined into the unknown. I didn't look back. She stayed back maybe waving her arms goodbye to love, tearfully. The dark haired girl slipped out of sight and fell through the grainy light of a hazy late morning. Yet, she clung to my mind. And, along with her smiling face, I was left with another thought clinging to my consciousness as I drove away in the truck. I could not decide if, by gracefully allowing me to leave her, she had done me a favor or if she was really the victim.

Chapter 13: LIMPOPO'S BONES

D id you see how this border's wire was cut into a large hole so as to make it easier for the illegal immigrants to go through the border? It's written in this newspaper, Sibusiso."

"Yes I saw it. It's in the Daily Sun of yesterday?" Sibusiso didn't usually want to watch issues about Zimbabwe on the television let alone read articles about Zimbabwe in the newspapers. He would grow angry while watching anything to do with the border and especially the Limpopo River. The tides of this transient river pulled his blood to a place which he didn't want to think on ever again.

"Yes, see that there. This border has become a place to explore people's initiative and creativity in successfully passing through into a foreign land illegally without being nabbed, I suppose.

Sibusiso barely even raised his eyes in acknowledgement.

They were lounging on bunk beds in a room they shared at a farm in the deep hot valleys of Thohoyandou in the Limpopo region, on the border with Zimbabwe. The soft and smooth bass guitar lines of a grey dove woven into the immediacy of the summer air slipped through the curtains and into their room....a dis-restful room, especially in the heat of a summer's day. It was late afternoon on a Sunday; they had been sharing that room for six months, but neither had talked much about how each got to be there.

The one who started the conversation, Chengetai, was the one who was the last to come to this farm. But, it was Sibusiso who had bought the newspapers from Thohoyandou, the previous day on a shopping trip. Chengetai thought Sibusiso was South African and, even though Sibusiso knew that this wasn't true -they were both Zimbabweans- what he didn't know was that they had come the same way to South Africa. Gathering a thought to himself in the languid moment, Sibusiso worked into his point artfully.

"I wish they would just remove that bloody visa. 2000 Rands is a lot of money and very few people can afford access to that kind of money in Zimbabwe. So many lives have been lost like fallen autumn's leaves, drifting downstream in Limpopo River. It wouldn't be all that...and a lot of lives would be saved...and guilt too if they were to remove that requirement."

Chengetai had looked at Sibusiso quizzically. There was always something secretively guilty about Sibusiso, as if he was afraid of something. Chengetai had always dismissed that and said to himself that it might have something to do with a family or personal issues. Nettle seeds need no germination; he had a lot of guilt feelings himself to deal with. He had left his girl in Zimbabwe, and had lied to her that he would be back in three months time. Now, it was almost eight months, give or take the month or so he had spend at the refugee camp in Musina processing his papers, since he had seen his dark-haired girl.

Chengetai was not even communicating well with that girl. In fact, he hadn't been phoning her regularly, but he still loved her. He sometimes felt lonely and missed her, but there was nothing he could do about it. Before leaving, he hadn't even told his family of his plan to cross the border to find a brighter future in South

Africa. And, he had enacted the plan so poorly...to start with: he had stolen the money he had been given to pay for his little brother's school fees and his uncle's cell phone. He used the money and the phone in a barter to get a ride into South Africa. He had since repaid the monies and bought his uncle a new cell phone to replace the one he had traded for transport to South Africa. But, he still felt guilty about the money he had stolen, money which should have paid for his little brother's school fees. That little brother had lost a full term's tuition because their mother didn't have more to pay for his fees that term.

"Life is a bundle of the impossibility...the difficulty, Sibusiso, but it is important like you said that we should try to save lives if we really can. Sometimes, it simply is impossible. Guilt rules our lives after that, after failing to save the lives that we could have saved had we tried a little bit.

"Yeah."

Sibusiso remained quiet, withdrawn. A shadow descended upon his face. Chengetai could see that Sibusiso was grappling with things he couldn't voice. The two of them had always worked as a pair, but most of the time silently. He had observed Sibusiso grappling with these things, with the shadows on his face when they were quiet. Sometimes, they would lock eyes and Sibusiso would smile just to remove the focus from discussing these things. When picking ripe oranges, they each had dealt separately and silently with their own private issues, but could talk the business of harvesting these oranges, exchanging ideas, but not about their private lives, no. All they had exchanged over the six months they had known each other were knowing glances and smiles. The language of communication between them was not a difficulty for both could speak very good English. Chengetai took the gamble this time and asked Sibusiso the question that had lingered between them for so long.

"Where in South Africa do you come from, Sibusiso?"

"You know that's the very funny thing about us, Chengetai. We have never talked much about that, you know. My friend, I am not South African."

"Don't tell me, Sibusiso! You are not South African? I thought you were, so you are from...Zimbabwe, are you?"

"Yes, I come from the Gwanda area. I suppose you assumed that, since I can speak most of the South African languages, it meant I was local?"

"I thought so, yes."

"You know it's easy to learn most of these languages if you are Ndebele. The languages relate somehow. There are common words and terms between my home language, Ndebele, and, Zulu, for instance. I have also been staying here for many years now."

"So, when did you come here?"

"I have been around for quite a long time, Chengetai. I came here after my grade seven, fourteen years ago. I didn't have money to continue with my studies in Zimbabwe so I came here. That's the only alternative I had." Sibusiso didn't want to explain anything further than that, but Chengetai wanted more.

"Hey, you have really been around. I have only been here for about 8 months. I still feel guilty of having to lie to my parents and my girlfriend about coming here. I also stole from my mother and uncle to make the journey here. But, coming here, getting across the river wasn't much of a problem, though. I paid a truck driver some money to smuggle me through the border through the legal entrance at Beitbridge. I had to spend a difficult month or so at the refugee camp in Musina processing my refugee papers. Tough world, the refugee camp is, but I am glad I am here now. I have repaid the money I stole and bought my uncle his replacement cell phone so I feel I have repaid a bit of the pain I made them go through. I only hope they don't hate and despise me anymore."

"We have to do whatever we have to sometimes, Chengetai, even when we don't really want to." Sibusiso said with a shrug.

Sibusiso still couldn't pronounce Shona words well; especially Chengetai's name which he still pronounced with a unique Ndebele perjink intonation. It wasn't only the pronunciation of his name that tugged some things in Chengetai's mind, though. It was that thick feeling of guilt in Sibusiso's voice again. He didn't need to probe more this time. Sibusiso became a bottle that had unstopped itself. "You know what…?"

"Yes, what Sibusiso?"

"I haven't spoken about my life before I came here to anyone really. I started working here a couple of years ago, but before that I did some terrible things, things that I am not proud of, some of the most terrible things one can do to a fellow human being."

Sibusiso took some heavy breaths, was quiet for some time. Chengetai didn't say anything. He reasoned that that was the best thing he could do. After some moment of silence, Sibusiso started talking. He told Chengetai everything of his coming to South Africa and his life before he took the job at this farm.

Sibusiso told him of his past as a Malaitshas (border gangsters) plying the border areas, helping people crossing over to South Africa illegally. He did everything bad when he was a Malaitshas; he stole his clients' money, and things they could be carrying, even abusing and beating up some of his clients. On one particular day, he helped a group of ten people to cross the Limpopo. At the crossing point, he told these people to follow right to the dot every one of his instructions. This group was an assortment of people, both Shona and Ndebele, young and old. He used Ndebele to tell them that they had to follow in his footsteps, putting their foot exactly where he had put his own foot. Sibusiso knew the river that well. He knew that a wrong footing meant instant death for those who couldn't swim that well. A couple of yards downstream, there was a very deep pool which was infested with crocodiles. The people had to hold each other's arm making a link against any attack from these marauding crocs.

In that group, there was a woman who had a two year old child. He offered to carry the child for her. This woman was the second last in this queue. All along the journey that woman had been such a hell hole, bickering and asking a lot of questions, but Sibusiso had sucked it up. He did this because the woman had been referred to him by his friend whom she was meeting in South Africa. This woman was that friend's girlfriend.

In the middle of the river, where the river was at its deepest, that woman lost her footing and fell, taking with her the last man in this queue. The water was a little bit higher in this river because it had rained for some days before that. The two were swept down the river whilst the rest of the group looked on. There was nothing anyone could do to save these two so they simply watched as the two tried to grapple with the water's strong currents pulling them into the crocodile infested pool. The little child started crying for his mother. Nobody seemed to hear the child.

Karma must have slept with the crocodiles. They watched

those two as the crocodiles tore them into pieces and feasted on their flesh. Nobody managed to walk. Everybody just stood in the middle of the river, entranced as they watched. They watched like they were listening to the sounds of the lute playing on the water's waves, not witnessing a massacre and watching the pool's water change to a red color from the blood of the two.

Sibusiso had to bellow aloud for the people still standing in the middle of the river to start moving. He told them they had to walk faster now; if they didn't do that, then they were going to be eaten by those crocs. The crocs were now exploring upriver for game. He knew they were now wild with hunger for human flesh and blood. He started wading furiously across this river knowing already that he was going to lose a lot of his clientele on this trip.

The lull it had taken them to watch the crocodiles feasting on those two was now their undoing. He didn't bother anymore about saving anyone, except his own skin. The crying child was an irritant. He simply ignored that little boy as the kid called for his mother.

"Sweet suffering Jesus! How many managed to cross to safety, Sibusiso?" Chengetai interrupted Sibusiso, entranced by this story - the epic proportions of the story - which seemed so alive in his mind. He was one of the illegal border crossers in the story, imagining himself walking behind Sibusiso, step by step, carefully as if matching his stride in the waves of the Limpopo. He pictured the shimmering morning sky bouncing madly across the bloodied ripples in the river. All that he remembered of the river was the river's brooding dirty dark waters as he crossed the river across the bridge tucked away in the truck.

"Only me, the child and two other girls managed to push through to the shores. After crossing the river, I told everyone to keep running into the forest. We ran into the bush, a bit far from the river. Chengetai, we ran in fear, our lungs aching and hot, our knees swelling, shins stubbing. Nobody waited to see how many more made it out of the river."

"Because you knew if you waited for the others by the river's banks the crocodiles would have followed you onto the banks of the river, Sibusiso?"

"Yes, that's why we didn't wait."

"So, what happened afterwards?"

"After waiting for an hour for someone to come through, it was getting lighter and lighter; it was about six in the morning. When I discovered that no one was coming through, I asked the two girls if they knew anything about the mother of the child. I lied. I told them that I didn't know anything about that woman and behaved as if I didn't know my friend was waiting for the two down in South Africa, as if they were people I had just met, as well. The girls said they didn't know anything about the woman, but that the woman said she knew me, and that her boyfriend was my friend. I told them she lied to them, that I didn't know anything about her. I knew they knew I was lying. I didn't want to have to take the responsibility for the kid anymore than I had already done. I told them I wanted to check the river to see if I could find anyone alive or for some information to help me access the relatives of the kid. I told them I would be returning back in a moment, that they had to wait for me."

He left for the river with the child. He left those two girls alone. The river was about a kilometer away. When he arrived at the river, there was no one alive. He dumped the kid near the river and took another route into South Africa. Walking off, he ignored that child's cries; he left the boy, the little two year old boy, there in the middle of nowhere. He didn't only abandon the child, but also those two girls in the middle of the deep dark forests.

Chengetai felt dumb; he was staring at Sibusiso as if he was staring at an alien being, at some extraterrestrial being light years ahead of him. He couldn't even bring himself to accuse Sibusiso of murder. He knew he didn't have to say anything, but to try to understand why someone would do that. Whatever guilt he felt about stealing his mother's money and the uncle's cell phone now paled in comparison to the guilt he knew Sibusiso felt for abandoning an innocent little soul and two harmless girls in the middle of nowhere.

Chengetai understood that Sibusiso knew the depths of guilt. The real depths are unfathomable. A weightless, a torrential kind of grief descended over him. His cartwheels through life meant nothing here where sadness and pain met. He told himself silently that, here is someone who has had to deal with the real human issues of illegal border crossing!

Chengetai couldn't sit on his bunk bed anymore so he stood up and made to the window. He needed fresh air to hit him. The sky to the east where the windows faced was turning purple, mottled and bruised by ruby clouds. He knew Sibusiso's bruise was the size of that sky.

"How did you keep sane after all that Sibusiso? If it was me, I could have gone bonkers, I should think."

"You learn to live with that kind of guilt and pain, Chengetai. Either you let it destroy you or you learn to live with it. For some time, I wasn't okay. I will be the first one to admit that I wasn't normal for some months after that. I phoned my friend and told him that I lost everyone I was helping to cross into South Africa, including the child and his woman. I had to phone him a couple more times to let him know I was so sorry, that I had done everything in my power to save everyone. My friend was inconsolable, but there was nothing more I could do. I couldn't reverse the situation, but guilt kept eating inside me. A week after that I began to have some scary dreams. At first, I could hear a child crying in my dreams, though I couldn't see him or stop him from crying. The sounds the child was making were similar to those of that child I had abandoned on the banks of the Limpopo. Later, the child's face began to be visible in my dreams. I would try to stop him from crying; telling him that his mother was coming very soon and that he should stop crying. I would feel the pain in his voice, on his face, the face that seemed not to see me, yet he was crying right before my eyes. I didn't know how to stop the child feeling the way he felt in the dream. It was so difficult for me. In my dream, I would end up calling for the mother's child to come back and take the child and stop him from crying. Then, some white shaped figure with a blared face would appear in the dream. She would tell me that I had to let her family know where I had abandoned the child so that they could collect his bones and bury them. She told me that she needed rest too and that the child was also persecuting her, and that the child needed to rest, as well. The spectre of the mother made it clear that I had to do something as soon as was possible to solve the situation before it got out of hand."

Chengetai felt the hairs on his head raising and curling up like question marks. Sibusiso also told him that the dreams would vary, but this crying child and a blared faced person always appeared.

The message was always the same. During the daylight hours, he persecuted himself as one of the guilty. During the day, he would deal in his mind with a family of the ghosts of the seven who had perished and the guilt of the two girls he abandoned in the forest. Every night, that whole damnable clan would show up in his consciousness and argue with him in his mind, each in his or her own dialect.

He told Chengetai that, if he had never heard ten or so people hurling and shouting insults at him in the mind in different languages, then he hadn't known what noise was. Eventually, he couldn't take it anymore so he phoned his friend and told him the real truth of the matter. Together, with that friend and some relatives of the child, they went to the border and searched for the child, a month after he had abandoned him. Sibusiso led them to the crossing point. They found the child's decaying decomposing body besides the river right where he had left him. They took the body to Zimbabwe illegally for burial.

The grave was not a refuge; the debt still remained. After paying a fine to the family of the child and woman and doing a traditional appeasement ceremony, he returned back to South Africa, applied for a refugee permit, looked for a job and got the one he had now as a farm worker, a couple of years ago. He told Chengetai that he never talked to or saw that friend of his again, that his friend said he didn't want to have anything to do with him anymore. He had also stopped being a Malaitshas as well.

"How do you feel about everything now, Sibusiso?"

"I still feel so terrible sometimes. I feel so sorry to the families of all the people I couldn't protect that day, especially for that small child who hadn't asked for anything in life, to whom I still feel I was culpable for his death, Chengetai. It's one of those things that I will have to live with for the rest of my life and take back with me when I die. There is nothing I can do to change that."

"I am so sorry, Sibusiso. I wish there is something I could do to soften the guilt and pain. But, you know, we have to forge on with our life, Sibusiso. We all have done a lot of things we are not proud of."

"I suppose so, but it's difficult." Sibusiso's voice seemed to be echoing through the damp halls of chilly Hades.

"Do you know what became of the two girls?"

"No I don't. I only hope they made it out of that forest which was rife with lions. I can only hope they survived those forests. That's the only thing I still hope happened. That's the only thing I could believe in so as to soften the guilt of their abandonment, Chengetai."

"Yes. I also hope they managed to find the way out, Sibusiso."

Chapter 14: GERMISTON 1401

He saw the light green stripes of the police's car flashing past him. He was at the intersection of Bailluel Street and Menin road. It was nearly the end of month. He knew the police did such a roaring trade at this time of the month working themselves to a standstill on foreigners, getting bribes on trivial mistakes. He cursed his luck when he saw the police's Volvo vehicle stopping, just ahead by the intersection.

Under his breath, he cursed himself for using Bailluel Street. He told himself he should have used Elsburg road, but he had decided against it because it, too, had a lot of police vehicles plying it. It was the main way out to Elsburg. He knew he had to face them anyway. They said, "Linjani Baba"

"Sikhona" was his reply, appropriately.

He tried to soften the pharyngeal fricative and pronounce "Sikhona," with less of the guttural tone of his language. They asked him where he was going and where he was coming from in the Sotho dialect. They knew there were very few foreigners who would know that glottal language. It was the most complex to learn.

When he failed to answer them, they smiled at each other. He knew those policemen were wolves waiting for a wrong word to descend upon their prey. They were still sitting pretty in their car which he thought to himself, was a good sign. Facing him with no faces, watching him with no eyes, he thought to himself.

They asked for his passport; he had it in his hands already. This thing of getting out his passport from his pockets before he was asked for it had become, to him, normal, even automatic. Whenever he saw a policeman or police vehicle passing by, he felt like stopping and waving his passport to absolve himself from this tremendous guilt he felt for being a foreigner in a land that didn't like foreigners.

This feeling had started some months before he and some of his friends were stopped by the police on their way to Johannesburg, just after the flyovers on M2. The police can be so abusive, sometimes. On that night, not long before, they were out to prove something.

They had asked for documents. He had left his passport at home that night. He couldn't produce any. The policemen accused them of being thieves, his reasoning stemmed that this must be the case since all of the passengers in the car were of different nationalities. His friend, Awilo Yambongo, was from the DRC, and his friend's friend, John Phiri, was from Malawi, whose friend, Kenneth Musanide, was from Zambia and he was from Zimbabwe. Those policemen told them to get out of the car with their hands up.

They were required to flash their documents with one hand whilst the other hand had to be spread on the car's roof; their legs were, likewise, expected to be spread out. The police had forced them against the car, their knees jammed against their testicles as they searched them. These policemen searched with a fierceness that only comes from a grudge, from a trapped, tepid, maddening anger. So eager to diffuse any threat to their peace of mind, they searched for the explosives, and terrorists, they knew were in the car, underneath the car, on those bodies, in those hearts, and in their speech.

They noticed that he wasn't holding his passport. When they asked him where his passport was, he told them he had left it at home. They laughed sarcastically. They asked him what his name was. He told one of them that his name was Chatindo. They asked whether he would be able to prove it. He knew he couldn't, since he didn't have any documentation. He said "no". They told his friends that they were going with him to the police station for repatriation to Lindela Repatriation Centre to begin the process of deporting him back to Mugabe. They emphasized that he would be deported back to Mugabe, not to Zimbabwe, as if Zimbabwe had been renamed Mugabe without his knowledge.

He knew what they implied and what they were trying to do. They were trying to scare him and to scare his friends. They told his friends to pay up if they didn't want him to be deported. His friends offered 100 Rands which they took, but refused to release him saying they needed more money. His friends added another 50 Rands which they took, though they still refused to release him demanding for still more money. He told his friends to let the police take him to the police station. His friends said they were not leaving him to those greedy bastards.

Other police cars plying the route sped past quickly. They never stopped to talk or to inquire what the matter was; they knew this was nothing more than another low-budget shakedown. His friends offered another 100 Rands which the policemen took, but still refused to let him free. Not knowing what else to do, his friends started haggling with these policemen. He felt like a house on auction. It was a feeling, a foul memory of another time long before his existence, which rotted inside of him. He knew it was wrong. A life should never be haggled over. A life is not a possession that can be traded, bought, or sold.

That's when an explosive started growing on his heart, refusing to be diffused, swelling, thundering and thundering inside his chest, in his heart. The accent of struggle got stuck in his mouth, deep down in his heart. He knew when not to open his mouth. He knew that, if he were to open his mouth, then he would have let loose expletives against these policemen. And, he knew that such language would end poorly, not just for himself, but for all of his friends there.

He kept silent as they haggled on his actual auction price. His friends haggled and haggled. When the policemen realized that they were not going to get anything more from his friends because they had turned inside-out his friends' wallets, they released him with a warning that he should always travel with his passport. After that encounter, that night, he and his friends had returned home for they no longer had the money to spend in Johannesburg. So it has come to pass that, since that night, he has wanted to show every policeman his passport.

Now, on this night, it had happened again. He had been singled out again by these policemen. Sure, maybe they were different police, but they still were the same. The routine was the same. The grudge was the same. These jackals asked him for the passport again. He gave them the passport. They scrutinized it as if it would miraculously become invalid. He could feel the hunger in their eyes for his passport to be illegal somehow. He knew he wasn't going to get out of this situation that easily. These policemen were broke and desperate. They returned his passport back to him when they found it was very much legal, but still asked for something. They wanted money.

When he asked them whatever for, they said that if he doesn't give them something, then they would simply take him to the police station and falsely detain him for some trumped up charge. They told him that he should pay them whatever he felt was enough for drinks. Knowing that they would follow through on their threats, he gave them the 30 Rand that he had in his wallet. He didn't want to spend a night in the police cells, so it was worth giving them every last bit of his money. They complained it was too little, but he told them he didn't have more.

They asked to search his wallet so he gave it to them. After they had meticulously searched the wallet's pockets and found nothing, they threw it in his face and insulted him, calling him a dirty makwerekwere (dirty scavenger). This was the derogatory name his countrymen were being called by the South Africans. Then, they drove off. He was angry, but there was nothing he could do about it other than suck it up. That was the game. He knew that all of this was nothing compared to what he had lived through. It was not his country, he reasoned. He didn't have the right to ask to be treated respectfully.

He had come to learn to deal with that kind of ill-treatment in his country of exile. He had come to accept that foreigners don't have rights in this country when he had been caught in the xenophobic mob attacks just two years earlier. Up to that time, he had been staying in a shack with his friend, Awilo, and a couple of other Zimbabweans. These were tight quarters with no comfort.

The four of them had shared one shack, no bed, and a couple of pots and plates. They were trying to build their lives in this country which they had escaped to just some four or so months before. They had been providing contractual work at the industries, mostly factories, in Primrose. The low wages and remote location of this industrial area forced them to stay in the infamous Ramaphosa settlement.

Ramaphosa was so insecure in those days. It remained insecure, but it wasn't his problem to deal with now. He had moved from there. In those days, he had counted himself lucky every morning when he had awakened alive. It was different with the area he was now staying, especially in Delville south. It wasn't a bad place, though there was tension. Delville south was predominantly occupied by the whites, while Delville north, where he was staying, was predominantly occupied by blacks. The wealth gaps between these areas that were in the same city and not more than one hundred miles from the other were obvious to anyone and everyone.

This white area had all the necessary trappings of wealth including tight security with several security cars doing twenty four hours patrol in the streets. Thinking back to his earlier encounter with the police, he remembered seeing an ADT car which had been following him ever since he entered Bailluel Street from Elsburg road. It was a good example of the tensions still brewing in the place. These security cars had taken over from apartheid police vehicles and were following black people around these suburbs as if every black person was a thief. While that security vehicle had passed him before the police car came through, he was quite sure in hindsight that it was that security car's driver who had called the police. It was a good thing that the police officers no longer cared about anything other than getting bribe money.

As he passed through the verdant lawns on the side of Germiston bowls club trying to access Elsburg road again, he couldn't help counting the sports grounds that occupied that valley. There were volleyball, basketball, tennis, rugby, cricket, football and swimming pool pitches covering that valley between the Delville south and Delville north suburbs.

He knew that, even though he was staying in that area, it was still not easy to access these grounds without having to deal with racism and exclusion. White children always had a head start over black kids, especially those who were staying in the informal settlements like Ramaphosa.

He also couldn't accept that he had almost paid for the ongoing tensions in this country with his own life just two years earlier. He remembered that fateful night. It was on 13 May when they heard a mob of black South Africans coming shouting and singing revolutionary songs against foreigners, telling the foreigners to go back to their countries. Luckily, he and his roommates had already heard about these mobs and their rampages on the radio a couple of days before.

When it started in Alexandria, north of Johannesburg, he and his roommates knew that it was just a matter of time before the vitriol spilled over to this area. They snuck, that night, into the dark backyard of their shack the moment they heard the noise. They were lucky that their shack was at the edge of this settlement. Between it and the police station was another valley, a dumping ground for waste by the settlers. They managed to sneak through the darkness and run for the police station before the crowds reached them.

When they arrived at the police station they reported this to the policemen on duty. They were told that the police station didn't have enough manpower and vehicles to deal with it. They slept on the police station's lawns with no blanket, even though the May nights were getting chilly. He reasoned that it was better to deal with the cold than to deal with the angry mobs of black people baying for his foreign blood. It was so painful for him to read in the newspapers about his neighbor who was burned to death, for nothing more than being a foreigner, for failing to identify the Zulu name for an elbow.

He also read in the newspaper that they were even killing or beating up South Africans of foreign origin, even those married to South Africans. To think that someone would douse someone with liquid paraffin, rim a tire around, and burn the person to death, just because the person was a foreigner was still difficult for him to process, even now. Seeing the images of his Mozambican friend and neighbor burning to ash in the middle of the road was still haunting and difficult to comprehend. That an entire civilized nation could become a nation of feral animals was beyond him.

He heard they were even threatening to invade the police station and kill all the foreigners who had taken refuge there. Upon that news, he left the police station and told Awilo that he was going to the Methodist church in Johannesburg where he had heard people were going. He knew it would be a little bit safer there.

Straight away, he left for Johannesburg alone. It was as far as his money could take him. He didn't have enough money to leave for his country. So, he stayed there for half a year, in the church where he had taken refuge. The numbers kept swelling at this church until at one point over three thousand people sought safety there. Water at the church was scoured at an outside tap, a single tap for the thousands there, a single bathroom for the thousands there, and a couple of toilets whose sorry shape scared off so many of the people sheltered there. A lot of them helped themselves in the streets surrounding the place. Crime, rape and diseases were some of the things they dealt with, as well. Yet, regardless of how terrible things seemed to be, he couldn't abide the thought of coming back to Germiston. And, even if he had wanted to, he didn't have enough money to go back to Zimbabwe, not to mention that he didn't know what to do if he was to go back to Zimbabwe. He knew that life was even more difficult in Zimbabwe.

It was Awilo who had come to the refugee camp in Johannesburg looking for him over six months ago. Awilo took him back to Germiston, helped him secure work at the security company in Elsburg where he was now working. Awilo was working at another factory in this area. He knew that, if it hadn't been for Awilo, he would still be at the refugee camp. These were the thoughts he had as he crossed Elsburg road at Delville swimming pool and entered the gates into Kwa Peter's residence, the place he was now staying.

He couldn't help realizing that it didn't feel strange as he entered those homesteads. He realized he was settling down in this area again despite all the other problems he had encountered. Even though he still looked misplaced sometimes and wore the displaced expatriate's expression as protection, this place was slowly becoming a home. And, with that thought, loneliness for his ancestral home filled him. And, on this cool night with his breath visible, his soul took flight for a brief moment and carried with it a message of hope to the heavens about all that Zimbabwe has been and might one day again be.

Chapter 15: Chitungwiza

You have to have a lazy mind for you to be a lazy person, like those blasted city council leaders in Tilcor road", he says that to himself as he jumps a ditch in the middle of a side road, full of sewage shit flowing from some broken or burst cistern or pipe, behind Tinaye funeral services parlor. The shit pools into a dam of some sort, just behind this building, and he has wondered whether it is because of the work of the dead resting in this parlor house who wants a swimming pool to swim off the heat and hotness of the hell they were confronting. These dead leaping and swimming like porpoises, slick out of the parlor house, into the sewage pond. Then the shit finds a small outlet, as it flows through the Zengeza 4 shopping centre, down into the Pagomba valley. The grounds around the shopping centre were laced with millions of cubic litres of sewer flowing off.

Pagomba is a valley he passes through every other day. Other times, it's everyday, especially when he is on the hunt of some project, and he has to access internet services to communicate with, it could be publishers, editors, etc... Takunda is 26, an artist; he would like to call himself an artist. A lot of people take him as a loafer, argumentative, lazy sickly person, and they evidenced this by saying he sleeps a lot. They think he sleeps the day off in his one room lodging in Tsuro road. Even him, he thinks he likes sleeping, but he is not sure he is lazy. He thinks the city council guys are the ones lazy because they pass, jumps on top of this flowing sewage river, on their way to these shops to buy their midmorning or lunch break food, yet they don't seem to have an idea on how to sort this sewage problem, once and for all.

It has been on and off for a year now. One week it is bursting and flowing off- and after some couple of weeks, the lazy council guys will stench off the flow. It would hold for a week, and then it would burst off and start flowing again. To Takunda, it has created an outlet for his creative mind. He has been taking photos of these sewage pools and dams, not only that but the restless streets of Chitungwiza, the dirty, the dumping grounds, how one has to circumvent piles of rubbish that were spilling into the streets; maybe as evidence that these city council guys were the real lazzies, not him. Sometimes he tells himself if he was a better artist he would have encompassed an image of a young man fishing in these ponds. And besides the man would be Kristina selling her snacks, sweets, popcorn on a cardboard, besides the road. It would really have completed the image in his mind.

"We are fishing in the sewage ponds of our existences." It was not after seeing the Zengeza 4 shopping centre sewer. It was after seeing the perennial Rufaro road sewer brewing shit into the air. The sewer pipes in the city of Chitungwiza, broken in the great inflation years, were now breaking up again, and filth was going into the waterways.

"I like your memaphors, as always." Kristina, his girlfriend for almost two years had said, very sure of what she was saying. Her eyes were low, not wide, were focused on Takunda.

"You mean metaphors." She would shrug off her shoulders, and with rueful laughter, would agree with him, "You know," her face assuming an all-purpose emoticon, frown. He would laugh with her, too. Around him, even though ignorant, she was as innocent as bunny rabbits with carrots.

Kristina was impregnated in the first year of her secondary education by a fellow form 1 student, dropped out of school, only to come back a couple of years later, and then she got impregnated again and she doesn't know who was the father. She had been sleeping around a lot and wrote her "O" levels fully pregnant and failed all the subjects. A couple of years later she started going to school again and before she had sat for her "O" levels again she got impregnated again, wrote her "O" levels and failed, at least this time with E grading in Shona and Religious studies, and the rest of the subjects were U grading. Then she briefly got married to the father of this kid, who had to inherit two other kids he didn't know how to take care of. In half a year he had run off to South Africa and left Kristina with her load of kids. Kristina was never the one to give up. Kristina simply had poor taste in men, always choosing the father who had abused and abandoned her and her mother in these men, so she chose those guys who would mistreat her. She was on it again over two year later, until Takunda had had enough of seeing his childhood sweetheart always bungling.

He blamed himself for all these bungling from Kristina. If he had been strong, if he had been man enough he should have helped her to avoid all these love escapades. If he had been truthful he should have told her how he felt toward her a long time ago, and would have stayed her from making a mess of her life. Two years ago he had mastered courage and told Kristina how he felt. For some weeks on end Kristina hadn't believed that he really meant it, but he had stayed put. It progressed from there: touching, kissing, loving…and now he was thinking of moving in with these guys.

Two years later, she had been his stead girlfriend. She had rewritten her "O" levels again, and failed, but he had helped her settle into a career as a street hawker. She was getting barely enough to take care of her three kids, the first of whom was now going to school. He helped as best as he could, supplementing his girlfriend's upkeep.

It's the last thought Takunda had on his mind, as he entered the Zengeza sub-police station. He had been applying for clearance to host choral competitions for the youths in the archdiocese of Harare, at their church. He was one of the organizers at his church.

"Good afternoon, Baba." Takunda greeted the officer at the desk.

"Good afternoon, Son. You are back again."

"Yes, I am", Takunda tried to be brave, and continued, "but I am representing St Mathias Catholic Church.., youths at our church are hosting the archdiocese's youths in a charity singing event at our church, in a couple of weeks, so we wanted to apply for a police clearance."

"Catholics…,mmm.., obviously there are many youths involved", and another police officer, on another desk, stopped logging details of a rape case, he had been attending to, as he bulleted his attention to this new quarry, "Obviously, you need a lot of manpower, young man. I am sure you learned your lessons from that clean up debacle." He concurred with his fellow. Takunda felt as if he was being stalked by vultures, who were faking an attitude over him to hide their real interests, money.

And another one barged in, "Youths are rowdy types, especially those who go to churches, this is what we have discovered in our service."

This was a curious assertion.

The one he had approached emphasized this greediness; "You need, at least 10 police officers on the ground."

The funny thing he hadn't even asked him how many would be attending the event, the state of the place that would be hosting the event, whether it required a lot of manpower.

"And how much are we going to pay for the more than 10 officers, sir."

"About 450 bucks."

"450! No! We can't even begin to afford that, sir."

Another officer, "The church has money, young man. Don't be stingy with what doesn't belong to you."

"But, it's a charity event, sir."

"But, money is involved…, and think of what would happen if there were going to be another riot again, in fact we shouldn't even be considering your request…, you already have blood on your hands, and we are trying to understand your cause, so try to meet us half way. Do you want the death of your fellow church mates on you?" *Who said they were going to be deaths. Do I always cause deaths?* Takunda asked himself, that police officer had made it such as if he was now cursed, and death was always stalking him.

"I am a peaceful person, sir; and we are church people. There is very little chance of a riot happening at the church."

"Young man, you have heard our conditions. Its either you pay upfront the 450 bucks and get the clearance or you are not getting our clearance, and thus you are banned from hosting your event."

Takunda left the police station fuming. He was frustrated with the way things were like in his Chitungwiza. There is nothing that gets done by the establishment. The police only care about lining their pockets. The councilors were another bunch. In his area, the councilor, councilor Mamwamba was from the ruling party, and the MP was from the opposition party, so they were always on each other's throat, trying to control things in the area. The same now obtained throughout his Chitungwiza. The councilor would approve construction of houses in waterways, and the MP would order the police to raze them to the ground. The MP would secure funding for servicing of the roads, the councilor will torpedo that, refusing to clear the project, and it was the people who were made to suffer.

We are a flagless army, and we are fighting a hopeless war!

He remembers about that sad event again. He had been regularly going to the Internet Café, like now. Takunda had personally initiated a cleanup campaign, focused on cleaning up his area, especially around the Zengeza 2 shopping centre. He had motivated many young people of his constituency to participate in this. Kristina had helped him, too. She did most of the follow ups with the council on approval papers he had applied. Takunda was doing the police clearance. He was regularly at Zengeza 4 shopping centre to access internet services so as to talk and garner support with the relevant people, like *Zimbabwe Environment Management* (ZEM). He also contacted a local paper, *Today's News*, to promote them and their cause, that had promised to feature them, but Takunda had his doubts with this paper. He had to be a politician to garner its interests.

He has always had doubts with the media in his country. It was this media that had been fueling the two polar camps in every facet of the country. The same editor, when she was still the entertainment editor of this newspaper had taken, and Takunda now wants to think *stole*, his book of photographs, promising him she would do a review, but never got to it. So many times he had queried her, but she had ignored him. This misunderstanding had started from the beginning of their contact. She wanted to interview him, and he didn't want to be interviewed. Instead, he wanted a review done on his book, and then later, an interview. Worse still it was a book of wildlife photographs of Zimbabwe, so not much political weight could have been wrought from doing such an interview, let alone the review, that's why she never did both. Takunda has come to realize the media in his country wanted something that would help them sell and impose their political ideologies and beliefs in your work or views, which his photos didn't have. Takunda knew the clean up was interesting, that's why the editor had un-regretfully accepted to cover it. At least this time she hadn't been naïve to ask,

"What qualifications do you have to pursue this field?"

It's how she had started the botched interview. Takunda got numb and couldn't reply her, maybe he should have asked her,

"What qualifications do you have to interview me, to torment me?"

No, he couldn't, because he felt stupid. It must be a simple question for her to start with that. Did she believe someone has got to have a master's degree in photography to snap photos? Takunda knew that's what a lot people were good at in his country, at looking at qualifications on the paper, and think it would mean they were capable and competent.

"This explains why my country has the best educated people on the entire continent but fail miserably in growing its economy and developing."

We have papers, and papers don't do the work, thus we have become cloudy limitations that never pass our grandmother's minds.

But, in a country that prided itself on papers, you needed all the relevant papers to be able to do anything you wanted to do. He thought of all that as he went to the city council from the police station, and this time, it was for a different cause. The church youths wanted to use the adjacent, disused land besides their church as a parking lot for their clientele during the competitions. He had also tried to interest the press, and this time he had tried the other camps' papers, *Cmetro*, and it had been a rollercoaster with that paper, as well.

When he first approached them formally, they had ignored him. So, he had decided to use someone who worked in the larger group of these newspapers, who was a driver of some executive there. This friend had helped him in getting the story to the editor. But this editor of *Cmetro* smelled money, so he had demanded for his cut. Despite being told that no money had rolled hands, he still expected his cut. The police were doing the same, saintly. The fun thing for him was that it was a charity event. He is boggled why both the press and police expected to be paid. It was the press that always surprised him.

In the cleanup campaign, the editor of *Today's News* hadn't even bothered to field a reporter to cover the clean up as she had promised. But after the riots she had bugged him for an interview, and came to police station several times to push him for an interview. She had also published unflattering things about him, when he had refused her the interview. She blamed him for the debacle because he hadn't acquired enough security to man the event. Not only this paper, a lot other papers asked him questions, asked to interview him, but he refused.

He didn't attend the mass for the singing competitions, he hates waking up early. He feels for him to function well he needs his sleep that's why he didn't even sleep at the church, like all the other youths had done, let alone coming early morning for the 7AM mass. He arrives at about 9 o'clock and hits the paths running around doing final touches, as the youths started arriving from all over the vast Harare archdiocese. He is not afraid they decided to only seek the clearance letter from the main police station at Makoni station, without seeking the quotation of police officers to secure the place that their local station wanted. It's a church event and they are church people who would be there, so there was no need to fear the debacle of over 6 months before. As he had learned when he worked as night watchman in Harare, over 6 years ago, security was mostly theatre. Your safety relies in protecting an authority you do not even have, so any acting experience you have becomes invaluable. So, at this church event he had decided to employ a couple of bully, heavy muscled guys to man the gates. Anyone coming in the gates would know the place was secured because those two bully guys were acting it out. This is what he had failed to do with the cleanup.

"I couldn't even cook the afternoon meal for my little kids, Takunda." Takunda remembers this conversation he had had with his then girlfriend Kristina, on their way to the cleanup.

"Why not Kris…, it's not too early. You should have done all that before coming. What were you doing with your early mornings?" Concerned for the welfare of kids, Takunda had asked her.

"There was no electricity, not enough money for gas or paraffin, Takunda. As you can see the firewood is even more expensive. Are things going to be changing any soon, babes? It's getting too hard for me to keep my head above the waters."

"Yah, things are just getting worse and worse. I can almost feel we are on the slippery slope of pre-2008."

"Aaaah, babes, 2008 ma one chaiwo (2008 is the difficulty one). It would kill me this time around." Kristina not sure of what else she can do if it were to deteriorate to that level, again.

"Don't worry; you have me this time around". Takunda had tried to assure Kristina, but he wasn't even sure now what he could really do to easy things with her.

Maybe, I should stay right there for her!

The two had talked as they made their way to Zengeza 2 shopping centre for the clean-up campaign. It wasn't far from where they stayed. Takunda was lodging a room in Tsuro Street, and Kristina with her kids, stayed on her deceased parents' property in Tsukukuviri crescent. The two were 3 streets off each other. They were walking, and were at the fringes of the shopping centre, in Jecha way. The way, which was a road-wide way was full of rubbish, especially off Mutsi street, where a mountain of rubbish had been accumulating, being dumped off by the Mutsi street residents. And, a little ahead, on the intersection of Jecha and Guyo Street, just in the lower skirts of Nyatsime beer hall, the dirty here was so bad. Combined with the broken durawall of the bear hall and the junk metals used to close off those breakages of the durawall, the sight was too ugly for anyone to have a second glance on it. This durawall had been broken down in the halcyon 1990s food riots when the police and army tried to beat the revelers in the beer hall. The drunken revelers had broken the durawall as they fled from the police's tear gas and button sticks. Jecha way at around that point was thinner such that the dirty had been floored into the road by cars passing through. The way was uneven also, with huge two potholes that had been accumulating rain water in this wet summer. The mixture of raw rubbish and rain decay in the street smelt so bad, with big worms, caterpillars and big flies wriggling from this mixture.

The two avoided entering the shopping centre by the off-road next to Guyo Street. They took the back road to the shops, came off the football pitch, and entered the shopping centre off the Main Musika Market. At the front of the main market they found other young people already grouped, waiting for them and the clean up to start. Takunda saw the eagerness that group of young people had, in the eagerness he finds in the young men coming from all over Harare for the competitions. It's a day out without parents for the lot of them, far away from their parish. It was going to be an opportunity to interact, which they don't find often. For a lot of these youths they were not interested in the actual singing, but just hanging out with other youths was enough.

At the cleanup point there was already a group of over 20 youths, exuberant and full of energy. And after a rather convoluted speech-prayer from one of the volunteers, they all trooped to behind the market, to clean up a huge pile of rubbish, off Njiva road. The people of the streets around Njiva had been piling up the dirty in this central place because the city council caterers hadn't been collecting rubbish in their streets, off to dispose it at the rubbish dump. These residents had decided to pile the rubbish at one place than to liter it around the streets.

The cleaners had just started shoveling, a few shovels of dirty, when a bully young man approached them, menacingly. Behind him trooped 50 plus other people, mostly ruling party thugs. Takunda was shocked to see Jekakwese leading them. Jekakwese was a hawker at the market place, did odd jobs, in and around the township. He wore faded blue jeans, torn by the knees, by life's tongue-slashing torment. He had always been a strong opposition supporter, over the years, but he was now with the ruling party. Takunda realized how things had changed with the last election. A lot of the opposition supporters had started deserting the party. The opposition was in shambles and consumed in leadership struggles, after another beating at the polls by the ruling party. In this group of the ruling party thugs was the well known, Madam Kunofiwa, people would finish off *Nokunakirwa*. Some called her Madam Kuno, some Madam, and some Ma. She was a local prostitute, very beautiful and attractive. She had 5 kids, each kid with his or her own father, prominent fathers. She was now with the councilor, or rather the suspended powerful councilor, councilor Mamwamba. Other than sleeping with the councilor, she was also the councilor's right hand woman. She knew who to buy to her cause and her body, though now full of HIV viruses, was always the draw card to any young men who was looking for immediate fun. It was obvious she had used her body to entice Jekakwese to her cause.

"I have orders from the councilor to stop this stupidity". Jekakwese started without any preamble.

"Why does the councilor or acting councilor want to stop it, Jekakwese? Takunda had asked him, his mind a wrench wench screwing the bolts of his anger ducts. It was the job of the council to cater off the dirty and keep the streets clean and it was frustrating to Takunda why the same people who were not doing their jobs would come back and try to stop those trying to help them. This said councilor should rather have been thankful to these cleaners because if he had been doing his job, rather than concentrating on enriching himself through hundreds of stands he had awarded himself, all over the city, the city and his area should be clean. This councilor was suspended from council work, so he had no right to stop or interfere with anything happening in the city. He had been suspended for corruption in the awarding of himself those stands.

"I have orders to stop it man, period! Do you understand me? I said I have orders." Jekakwese maintained his stance.

"Where are the orders?" Takunda asked him

"Its verbal orders! Don't you see my mouth saying it?"

"Yah, I can see it moving, but that is not how it works. I am sure you know that."

"Works where? The councilor said I should stop this tomfoolery, so I am stopping it. You think your western friends who publish those stupid photos of yours can just butt in our local homes and tell us we are dirty, and give you money to tell us we are dirty, and you expect us to just nod our heads in agreement."

"Unlike you man, who seems to be bought..." Takunda stopped and looked at Madam to point to him whom he thought had bought him "...We are not getting money from anyone for this. Use your eyes man. What do you see there, behind me? Is that not a mountain of rubbish? You see there, there are no western friends there, only rubbish..." Takunda had emphasized by pointing on the heap. "So what's with this nonsense about being paid, or no dirty, as if you don't see it yourself?"

"I don't give a damn, man. This cleanup is unauthorized."

"How can you say that when we have full council approval and clearance." He waved the clearance into the air. "We also have police clearance to do it, too, and bodies like Zimbabwe Environment Management knows of it and have provided all these tools we are using to do the cleanup."

"I told you I don't care. You might have an approval from your Pope you pray at the Roman Catholic Church but I still wouldn't care a hoot. The councilor, through the acting councilor has told us to stop it. You guys should have come through the structures of the party. The councilor should have been party of this campaign."

"This is not a political endeavor."

"The councilor owns this place." Madam had said. Takunda thought she would have loved to say she owned the place through her sleeping with the councilor. Rather, he replied her, correctly.

"Owns how…we elected him."

Jekakwese came to Madam's help. "So what…there is nothing that is not political in Zimbabwe. Everything is political. Even your cleanup is political. I am told you even invited the press to cover it. If it was not political, why did you invite the press, and why the trash paper."

"It is not even the political editor we invited. In case you haven't done your homework well, it is the community editor we invited, and this is a community event. So, we are continuing with the cleanup. You can watch if you want or get involved, whichever way, we don't give a damn, as well." Those were spitfire words, from Takunda, in sputtering ocher anger.

"You are a fool man. This is out of your depth. Quit before you create bloodshed here." Jekakwese had stepped back and he conferred with Madam.

The two argued for some minutes whilst the rest of their gang looked on, waiting for orders. Takunda and his friends had continued doing their job. A little later, Madam had conferred with the said councilor on the line, and then she came back with her new orders. She relayed them to Jekakwese. Jekakwese summoned the group together and imparted the instructions. The two, Jekakwese and Madam, had left off, leaving the thugs on the scene.

Five minutes after they had left, and from several corners of the shopping centre sprouted more youths, as if they were coming from the dirty that littered Chitungwiza, and several traders at this shopping centre and other onlookers gathered, too.

One of the thugs threw a half brick and hit one of the cleaners on the head, and he collapsed onto the rubbish heap, to add up to it. Before the cleaners could process it, more stones and bricks flew their way like cannonballs. Some cleaners ran off a bit, and the rest reacted and fought back. They attacked these thugs with a motley lot of tools they had; picks, shovels, hoes, brooms, and wheelbarrows which were rammed into the thugs' feet and legs. The battlefields thickened with the new arrivals, and then the onlookers entered on the side of the cleaners. It was kill or be killed. As the fighting continued and casualties mounted, it became about protecting those whom one knows, so Takunda tried by all means to protect his girlfriend Kristina, and Kristina protected him in return. He hoped she didn't mind being given third degree wounds on her body.

As more people piled up on the ground, some dead, some nursing life threatening injuries, some barely hanging on their feet, fighting; the police came, thirty minutes after the fighting had broken out and stopped the fighting. They arrested everyone at the scene. The ambulance carted off the injured and the dead to the hospital. Takunda and Kristina had been arrested with the others. To Takunda, even the heavens seemed broken open.

Six months now, his life had gone through hell. His relationship with Kristina wasn't that tight. They had gone through the hell together, but rather than binding them together, the trails had pulled them apart. They had drifted badly. What brought this breakdown was when Kristina was jailed; her kids were left with no one to take care of them. The next door neighbor tried all her best to help out, but the time it took for their case to be cleared by the courts, over 3 months, wrenched its toll on the kids. It made them major into what it means to be adults. Kristina blamed herself for that, thus Takunda knew that deep down she blamed him, too. She never said it but Takunda saw the pain mirrored in his eyes, a chemistry that he knew well in his heart. He blamed himself, too. What galled Takunda was the loss of life that he felt he was personally responsible, and this made him withdrew into himself, too. Those ten people who had died, he still felt he was responsible for. It had been his idea to do the clean up, and it was him who had motivated these to join.

Worse still, those that had caused that to happen, Jekakwese and Madam had been released from police custody, two hours after they had been arrested. He still feels soul-cutting knife anger when he meets these in the streets. They had denied they had given the thugs instructions to attack the cleaners, but had left them to guard

122

these cleaners. They changed and twisted the conversations they had with Takunda before the fight. In fact, they now maintained the councilor was in full support of the cleanup endeavor, and that they had encouraged those who had attacked the cleaners to help the cleaners. The councilor had posted bail for these two, and in matter of two hours, they were scotch free. Yet the likes of Takunda and Kristina had to spend 3 months in police custody, waiting for trail.

Even though a number of the thugs had been convicted of inciting violence and disorder, Takunda still felt it had all been a joke, the trail and sentence.

But, he was never the person to give up, so when he was approached by the other youths at the church, a month out of police custody, cleared of all the charges, he accepted this new cause. The weight of those deaths, in his lonely moments was too heavy for him. He would hear vertical voices; these were always the images that would haunt him, until he slid down a shaft to the bottom of sleep. But now, every morning he would soldier on.

If you want a taste of freedom, keep going, no matter what! It was now his new mantra.

"Takunda, here is the girl I told you asks about you, every time I see her."

"Oh….aah…hellooo." He had greeted her.

A sweet slim girl, with petite features, very pretty. His friend, Patience, had told him of this girl, and that the girl always asks after him. This girl had come to their church, a number of years before and had taken a fancy on him.

Now, he had finally met her, and he wasn't disappointed. It was a fine choral choir competition day, and the youths were enjoying it, and so, he tried to enjoy the day, as well.

He makes good conversations with the girl, for pretty much of the rest of the day.

Chapter 16: OPERATION *MURAMBATSVINA*

The bus in the early morning highway road had been gliding along like an ice skater. Nothing was challenging its stately, near silent traversing of the highway's arteries. And then, the bus driver reduced speed instantly. He was feeling sleepy, so he had been functioning between being sleepy and being fully awake, for some couple of kilometres of the journey. They were just ahead of Mvurachena Shops on their way to Harare, where Tyson worked. Mvurachena Shops are a couple of shops, and a gas garage on one side of the stream. On the other side of the stream was a mushrooming informal industrial settlement. Its growth, for a couple of years, had been phenomenal, to say the least. To its left was the Harare International Airport and right across, a bit ahead, were the gates to Manyame Air Base.

Tyson was surprised when the bus slowed down since there was no bus stop nearby. He drifted back from sleepy to fully awake. Inside the bus was warmer, though outside it was cold and chilly. It was fast approaching mid-winter, in early June. Everybody in the bus woke up. It started with those who were in the front seats saying "oh!", "oh!", "oh!", and another said, "look at that!" Tyson looked at it.

Another said, "What's the matter?"

Another asked, "Where are those police and army vehicles going?"

Someone said, "Oh, there are a couple of bulldozers in the middle!" That's what he was seeing, as well.

The road shook as the three bulldozers in the middle groaned and screeched like angry monsters, shuddering past them, keeping to the right side of this four-way highway between Harare and Chitungwiza. Those bulldozers were the ones being guarded by an entourage of police and army vehicles.

Another person joked, "Uncle Bob is now travelling in bulldozers these days."

People laughed for Uncle Bob jokes always made people laugh, and lift their spirits a bit. But, everyone in this bus knew that wherever that entourage of vehicles was heading towards, it had something to do with Uncle Bob in the jokes, and something that was devastating, at that. Everything to do with Uncle Bob was always like that. Tyson had argued, a couple of days before, with a workmate, Mr Marombe, about these things to do with Uncle Bob. He had asked him the question he always liked to ask people about Uncle Bob, especially those he knew supported the old man.

"For how long, do you want the old man to keep messing things for us?" Tyson had asked Mr. Marombe.

"He is not messing things. It's the whites and the MDC who have been messing things here." Mr. Marombe rejected the notion.

The funny thing was to realise each and every supporter of Uncle Bob was replying that question the same way, as if they had become robots and were now functioning as a collective consciousness of some sort. Mr Marombe had always disagreed with Tyson on that. He was a C.I.O (Central Intelligence Organisation) agent, based in the president's office. He always blindly supported the president and the ZANU-PF, against any criticism whether justified or not. The other workers at the company always wanted to provoke for that, but a lot were afraid of Mr. Marombe. Tyson enjoyed arguing with him. He knew he never took him seriously though. Mr Marombe just thought Tyson liked to disagree with him. Mr Marombe seemed to enjoy the arguments, as well. The two were very close at this company, ABC Motors. They covered for each other, several times, against the other managers. Mr Marombe had covered for Tyson, even with his own manager. Tyson would cover for him, doing most of Mr. Marombe's work whilst he concentrated on his private businesses- a farm, shops and political meetings. The other managers at this company were afraid of Mr. Marombe. He played truant with them. He had a climate considered tropical and the rains may fall as an all-day with him. He was also the chairman of the notorious war veterans, of Harare Province. Nobody would dare pissing him.

"What have the whites done? Hey, they never stole an election. It's Uncle Bob who did that. They never stole money, the nation's coffers for their personal use. It's Uncle Bob and his bunch of kleptomaniac coterie who did that, not the whites, not the MDC, no!"

Tyson wasn't scared of him, so he fought him head on. Maybe he liked the fact that Tyson was blunt and wasn't afraid of him.

"You don't know anything about this country, young man." He went on the defensive, and once he was set on that mode, there was nothing, no argument that could get through to him. He would become very belligerent in this comments field.

"We fought for this country, young man, that bunch of crooks you talked about deserves a pie of this country's wealth, young man. We didn't go to war so that the likes of you, young people, young kids at that, and the MDC and the whites could take our hard won independence and country from us. You have never seen anything, young man, about ZANU-PF. You are going to see what we are going to unleash, especially on the likes of you; young fools who think they know so much about life. Just wait and see, and then you will realise that it's the ZANU-PF that runs this country."

He had said that so confidently, even with a streak of arrogance and nonchalance. Tyson knew something huge was planned by ZANU-PF. Mr Marombe always told them things before they happened, but it was now quite obvious that he didn't want to do that, and so, Tyson tried to probe him, a bit more.

"What's going to happen, Mr. Marombe?"

"No, I am not telling this time."

"Why not?" Tyson asked.

"Because, it's a classified secret, Tyson, so you just wait and see, young man." He knew he wasn't going to extract anything more from Mr Marombe, so he left him at that.

When that entourage of police, soldiers and bulldozers had passed them, people started to question each other, in the bus; whether there was a strike in Chitungwiza, which they hadn't heard of that morning. Why were the police and army with their armoured vehicles going to Chitungwiza? Tyson didn't know, why? Nobody in this bus journey knew anything. But, when he arrived at his workplace, it was the same story coming with workmates who were from different high density townships of Harare. And, the feeling inside him was unshiftable; it gave off fractures; of anguish, of misplacement and of a scored emptiness. So, he went to check with Mr. Marombe what those trucks had been about. Mr Marombe was in such a good mood. He laughed sardonically when Tyson asked him about that, but only replied that he had warned him before, a couple of days before.

"So, what are they going to do in Chitungwiza, Mr Marombe?"

"You haven't figured that out, young man."

"No!" Tyson answered.

Mr Marombe laughed and said that he had to wait and find out what they were going to do in Chitungwiza and, by God; he was even having fun! It was not difficult to even think that his name wasn't Tyson, but young man, when he was talking to Mr. Marombe for he always called him young man. Tyson didn't know and understand what all that meant but he said, "I see!"

It was at about ten in the morning when news began to filter through from several townships of Harare and Chitungwiza. Everything became clearer and clearer by about afternoon. Those bulldozers, with the army and police protection, were destroying all the illegal structures in these townships, structures which were occupied by the poorest of the cities' people. That mid-morning news started filtering through of the destruction of people's *Boy's Skies* (that's the name they gave to those illegal shacks or brick dwellings they occupied in Harare and Chitungwiza), illegal truck shops and illegal buildings, mostly in the high density areas.

That afternoon, in the news, on the radios, the government had spoken of this operation and aptly named it, *Operation Murambatsvina* (that is, operation clean-up), and cleaning up what? The city's poor! Everyone knew why the operation was ongoing. These township people had voted against the president in the previous elections such that most of the cities in the country were now under the MDC rule and control. The operation was Uncle Bob's ill-conceived idea to displace this huge swell of support for Tsvangirai and the MDC, to punish them for rejecting him.

Tyson asked for the afternoon off from his boss, Mr Rusere, so that he could go and help his wife to salvage their things before the illegal structure that they occupied was destroyed with their properties inside. Mr Rusere told him that he couldn't give him the time off because it was affecting everyone at the company. They might as well end up closing the entire company to allow everyone some time-off to deal with the situation. There was nothing he could do about that. He couldn't have played truant with his boss and left his workplace without permission. He didn't want to lose his job, as well.

His wife phoned him early in the afternoons. He couldn't decipher what she was saying. She was crying, mumbling, saying "Tyson", "Tyson", several times; groaning and trying to say something but failing and gaggling. She had entered her fiefdom; talking whilst crying. There was also a huge swell of noise from people in the background, sounds of the graders boring into their illegal structure. He knew what that meant. He told her to take care of the kids and not to worry, and that he will be home by about night's fall. Tyson had to cut the call. He couldn't take anymore of her crying for her moans were too urgent in their pain, the words half formed as if stuck in her throat. They worked for the whole of that day like numbed robots. Everyone was silent and brooding and everyone felt hard done. Some people cried and some enthused that maybe their own structures hadn't been destroyed. A dark shadow descended upon everyone, though.

On the journey back home, Tyson got a whiff of what to expect in Chitungwiza when he saw the informal industrial settlement of Mvurachena on the ground. Some rubble of a people was huddling besides the road. They looked like they were posing for an event to raise some funds for the humans. Some people in this bus journey groaned with pain. Everyone was so scared of what they were going to see in Chitungwiza. Tyson's home was in Zengeza 1 Township, the core houses area, which is on the fringes of Chitungwiza. The area you would first touch as you enter Chitungwiza from Harare.

His body turned into granite when he first had a glimpse of his township. The place had basically been razed down. Just a few houses that didn't have some outside structures were still standing. All the other houses that had other structures were floored, despite the fact that most of these structures were legal and that the original houses were legal. Dusty and smoke swirled up and hung in the skies. At first he almost thought it was a funeral lamentation, and yes it was people who were crying, women, older people, young people, and some children; calling out to the heavens in the long notes, in trying to see if their gestures would illicit an answer. Their properties were outside and some were huddled together for warmth. They had nowhere to go now, nowhere to hide from the winter's colds. Boulders of broken concrete rubble and bricks littered the entire landscape, a place that had housed all those thousands of people who were now along the streets and on the main roads. Some were looking for cheaper transport that could take them to their rural homes where they could find shelter, some to relatives in some other parts of the city or in Harare. Tyson had nowhere to go other than to his rural home which was too far away and needed a lot of transport monies to get him there, the money that he didn't have.

Some streets simply vanished, leaving fields of concrete and bricks. They were also gap-toothed buildings and the music and laughter had gone too. He sat down near the bus stop where he had disembarked the bus and wept for minutes. And then, he proceeded to his street to find his family.

He found his wife in the street right across the place they used to call their home which was now debris and concrete boulders. Their cottage was surely floored. His two little kids were huddling for warmth in a blanket his wife salvaged. She also salvaged some pots and plates, clothes and other small utensils. The television set, radio, DVD player, wooden drawers and the bed had been destroyed. The sight was almost surreal like some part in a cataclysmic film. There was nothing he could say to his children, nothing he could say to his wife. He just felt he let them down. He couldn't look into their eyes. He couldn't watch the pain in their eyes. He knew he just couldn't take it. But, he still sensed the arching sadness behind his wife's unsmiling face, the insecurity and fear in his two boys' bearing.

He helped his wife quietly salvage the things. In the distances, the bulldozers were still rummaging the remaining houses in the township, guarded by a fully armed police and army and nearby, little boy-men, girls and little kids looked-on, over the street, at the houses being dug up, now full of pits and cracks.

He salvaged the bed, and beat it into shape, so also the drawers. The electronic gadgets needed a bit more fixing. That night with thousands other families they lighted the fires on the fringes of the street roads, cooked on the fire and slept in June's freezing colds, outside. Whole families were made homeless and slept outside in the winter's colds. They knew they had to figure out and work out their own problems because there was no help coming from the government. It was the instigator here. Their own government had granted them the freedom of the gutters, and deep in the gutters of Chitungwiza, they were now few gods, and all were people.

They slept for a week in the winter's deep penetrating colds. Every day when dusk crept from the night's hidden lair, the shadows would emerge, gripping his mind and his night's ritual would begin, sleeping in the dark, the sky polishing the stars, staring at those stars, trying to coax sleep; also staring at the empty spaces where his home used to be. Those dark night skies were always an immense lake, and the stars above the piled-up dark, if they remembered about him, they did not tell; were always like little boats navigating high above his head, wondering into the expanse of the sky as if searching for what was lost. Some stars were like clusters of lime and orange in a glass. The western sky seemed full of star-sweepings, piles of litter heaped up on that corner of heaven's floor, a litter of tinsel left over from an angel's party. And, he would wait for daybreak, watching this sky anxiously, so that daylight might give new translations to the whispers of these stars. It was almost devotion, this waiting of daybreak and daybreak; like crystals mesmerising his eyes, would arrive slowly and late.

During the weekends when he did not have to go to work, he would sit on a stone in the street right across another homeless fellow, caked in dirty and resting by the avocado tree.

The more the days passed the more those bulldozers destroyed the whole city, razing all the structures thought to be illegal. So that Chitungwiza of mile long streets, of sometimes muddy, black-muddy-waste streets, disappeared. That Chitungwiza of a grim and original beauty simply vanished. That Chitungwiza, the romance of which had always attended to the alchemic process of skilled transmuting labour disappeared, too. The teenage clatter crackling in the air like spring-time birds, blind with optimism disappeared. The kids who had played together since diapers days and became old man together parted. That was now their city with rotting corpses, bloodstained clothes, where the real heroes died out in the cold with no place to call home.

At the end of that week Tyson gave his wife some money for transport to his rural home, after he had applied for an advance at the company. She left with the kids for his rural home, in Hurungwe, with some of the things that they had salvaged and repaired. He crushed in with a friend who hadn't suffered the same fate.

*****

This aptly entitled "Operation Murambatsvina" program made over 700 000 people to become homeless in Zimbabwe's cities. It later became known as "Operation Zvipwanyire Wega" (operation destroy it yourself), after people took it over from the government and started doing the destruction themselves of their own illegal structures. If they had waited for the government's destroyers they would have lost possessions like furniture and kitchen utensils in the government's utterly insensitive drive. The government's drive didn't care about what was inside those structures. The graders just struck the structures and a number of people had died in this government's drive, so to be on the safe side, you had to destroy it yourself.

Chapter 17: Notes from Mai Mujuru's breast

They were busy digging when all of a sudden the police dog was upon them. It was a huge wild animal baring its fangs in Chris's face, baying for his warm blood. Chris tried to fend it off but it got his hand in its jaws. Chris bellowed with pain. Daniel had run on but when he heard Chris crying he stopped and turned to look back. He catapulted back into the battle lines without a thought for his own safety, grabbed a stick and beat the dog on its hind legs. The dog yelped as it let go of Chris's hand. Chris was up in an instant; he picked up his pack of soil and ran on towards the mountains. The police were now behind them, chasing them. They ran harder, but Chris was not such a good runner so the dog rammed into him before he could get clear. He fell down in a heap and the dog was on top of him, trying to bite his throat, but Chris was fast this time. He gripped the dog's neck. He couldn't crush his hand around its throat to suffocate it and barely held it off as they wrestled on the ground.

When Daniel realised that Chris was going to be devoured by this monster he dropped his pack of soil where he was, grabbed a big stone and made for the battle fields again. When he was near he took aim at the police dog and let the stone go in one powerful throw and the dog collapsed beside Chris. As Chris tried to rise from his position he heard the *cluck cluck boom* of an AK47 nearby. He looked around and saw Daniel sliding down as the bullets burned into him.

He knew that if he tried to run he would be dead meat, so he started slithering along the ground like a snake, gripping handfuls of grass, roots and rubble. It was a distance of 50 metres to the forest; he pushed through like a possessed man. Some would have given up, but Chris had to survive to tell the story, for Daniel and the other people who had died at the hands of the police here in Marange. He felt the darkness enveloping him. It was night; it seemed he was really dreaming...

He had survived before in this place. Five years ago, he was a young, level-headed man when his girlfriend Concillia asked to meet him under the baobab tree, in the western fields of Marange. They were out there for their annual Passover. It was their spiritual home, where their church originated, so every year they would make a pilgrimage to this area. He had grown up in this church, and found love in it. He and Concillia had promised to marry each other after this Passover. They were hoping for a revelation from God on their impending marriage.

As he was walking towards the fields that morning, he couldn't help noticing winter was setting in, colouring everything a grey, brownish colour, and the fields were bare of crops. Winter always made him feel anxious, as if he was about to lose everything, or maybe it was the tone in Concillia's voice.

"I want to talk to you, Chris."

"Talk? About what, Concy?"

"I think we should stop seeing each other. It's God's revelation."

"We haven't consulted the prophet. I don't understand you, Concillia."

"There is something that happened to me yesterday, Chris. I was praying under this tree in the morning, as I had been told to do by Prophet Madzibaba Johanne Wechipiri. In the church, last

Saturday, he prophesied to me that I should go to the Baobab tree and pray for our relationship. He said God would give me a revelation. I did as I had been told and was praying fervently when God bellowed in a huge voice from up the tree, telling me: 'Your prayers are heard, young woman.' I replied, 'Say what you want to say, God, your servant is listening.'"

"How did you know it was God speaking?" asked Chris.

"It was God, speaking in the voice of our Prophet Madzibaba Johanne Wechipiri."

"What if it was Madzibaba himself speaking?"

"No. it was God, God speaks through prophets, Chris. Please stop blaspheming the spirit of God."

Contritely, he asked her, "And what did he say?"

"He told me I was set aside for a great promise. I was going to conceive a prophet for the church; and this son of mine will be the son of the current prophet, Prophet Madzibaba Wechipiri. So, Chris, I have to marry the prophet."

Now, as he drifted in the dream, he saw Concillia. She was pregnant, and it was with the third child in five years, but she was groaning and groaning. Maybe he felt her groans in his own groans. She was struggling to give birth and his mind told him she was dying. He didn't feel he had to save her. There was nothing he could do about it all.

When Chris realised that he had lost his love to the prophet he was so devastated that he stopped going to the church altogether and started drinking himself crazy. His best friend Daniel told him he had to let go, but he couldn't. He knew deep down there was a conspiracy. Young men in this church had always been second choice to girls. Young people were not allowed to be prophets. Even when they were in the church, the girls were told to sit facing the old married men, whilst the boys and young men were told to sit facing old women. Daniel had also had his girl taken; now it was Chris's turn.

After the end of the pilgrimage, their group left for Nyatate, but Chris didn't go back with them. Even though Daniel tried to convince him to go back with others he refused. He parted with his friend. He stayed on in Marange. A couple of months later, when he realised he had no recourse with God, and that he was drinking himself into a wreck, he left for the city of Harare to stay with his uncle. He also started dealing with the drinking bouts.

Over the following five years, he drifted from one relationship to another, one job to another. This was now the situation; it seemed, of the whole country. He didn't have money, but nobody had money. It was at the height of the political problems in the country. People were scuttling all over the country trying to eke out an existence- not surviving, no. One couldn't even think of living, no. One just had to exist.

When he came to, Chris was on his stomach at the edge of the mountain. Everything was quiet. He touched his throbbing hand and remembered what had happened. He rose slowly, afraid of attracting those bloody dogs and the police. He looked down to the killing fields below and when he was sure there was no one there he started walking back to where they had killed Daniel.

Marange had changed him again. Growing up, this name Marange had meant something totally different to Chris. It had meant something so pure, so holy.

But Marange is a wilderness. In actual fact, Marange is a bloody pit. The hot air blows like a stoked blast furnace year round. You can't grow crops other than Rapoko and Mhunga, which sometimes don't get beyond germination. When diamonds were discovered the whole community thought it was a spiritual gift for the people of Marange as absolution for the recurring droughts in this place. For some time, they were inhospitable to people coming from other areas. But it didn't take too long before it became a Mecca for the rest of the country. Then the authorities butted in, in their usual grab-and-plunder way.

A few months before the whole country descended on it, those Johanne Marange Sect members had returned to Marange for their annual Passover. It was at the height of the Cholera epidemic that swept through the country. It wiped out Chris's family members. Now, he was back here too: but not to exhume the bones of his family members buried in Marange soils, no.

Chris phoned his old friend Daniel when he decided to take this journey and asked him to join him in the endeavour. Daniel had agreed, but mostly because he just wanted to see his friend, whom he hadn't seen in over five years.

He had taken a train to Mutare to meet Daniel so that they would approach Marange from the side which was less guarded, rather than the direct road from Harare. They were taken by a big truck to Chipinge, and then ferried on to Chakohwa. Then they walked on foot, a distance of over 50 km, crossed Odzi River and arrived at Marange at about six in the evening. On the way, they plotted their adventure together.

"Those guys over there are saying, the whole place, the whole Marange diamonds fields, has been parcelled into four parts. The first part is known as Mufakose." They were reclining under a hulking Mimosa Tree, off the road, across from Chiadzwa Shops. Mufakose literary means, "to die or suffer loss in everything", thought Daniel but he said:

"Yes, this is the place where we get the *ngodas*." A *ngoda* is a poor, cheap form of diamonds, an "industrial" diamond.

"Like Mufakose Township hugs the industrial area in Harare!" Daniel quipped.

"It hugs the industries for sure."

"Behind that river, they are saying that place is known as Mbare." Also named after the notorious high density slum of Harare.

They were waiting for the night to fall so that they could invade the fields with the others sleeping, loitering, talking, all around Chiadzwa Shops. They knew they could only get into those two places, Mufakose and Mbare. There were two other parts they couldn't invade. The third part was known as Mbada, named after the leopard, perhaps because of the beauty of the "glass" diamond found in this spot. The fourth part was known as Zamu raMai Mujuru: "Mai Mujuru's breast". The Mujuru family were mining this area. Chris and Daniel couldn't help laughing at this: the people still had a sense of humour. But another thought came to Chris's mind. A breast to a little kid or even to an old man represents life, living, loving.

Mbada Area and Mai Mujuru's breast were fenced off, with the police, the army, the intelligence, and the Green bombers doing 24hr guarding of the place. The police didn't want anyone near Mai

140

Mujuru's breast, and Mufakose and Mbare were too close. The government wanted everyone to go back to the actual Mufakose and Mbare Townships, in Harare, over 300 km away. So the battles in Mufakose were like a country at war. Chris, Daniel and the other people would stay away from the area during the day, and sleep at the nearby Chiadzwa Shops. A lot of people were killed; in fact, while Chris was there he witnessed at least 5 deaths every day. People were also being beaten up by the police; some were eaten alive by the police's dogs. Some had devised a new method to deal with the dogs. When they were being chased they would lead the dogs far away from the police, and then they would stone the dogs to death or give them poisoned meat. And the battles continued.

But still, everyone kept digging in the Mufakose or Mbare areas. The whole country was staying in Mufakose, mining whatever little *ngodas* they could scrounge, eking out an existence. But some poor people developed ambitions. Some couldn't abide the idea of staying in Mufakose for the rest of their lives.

And what did they do about it? They started foraging beyond the pig-fence wire that surrounded Mai Mujuru's breast. Inside the fence, *Zamu raMai Mujuru* was made up of heaped up mounds of the coveted glass diamond and soil. If you were to lick a bit of that breast, you would go home smiling and vault yourself out the Mufakose Township into the lush, leafy northern suburbs of Harare.

"So Chris, are we going to taste Mai Mujuru's huge mounds?" Daniel asked.

"We don't have the money to bribe the police on duty," said Chris. "It isn't possible for everyone, man. The sums they are demanding are so huge." One policemen was found with US$44

000 after an 8 hrs guarding duty. There was a lot of money involved. Chris and Daniel had used up everything they had on transport from home.

What it meant for them, and for most Mufakose residents, was that they had to stay down there, beside the industries with the "industrial" diamonds. For those with the money, they would be given under an hour to get in, through the gates or by cutting the wire, grab a piece of Mai Mujuru's breast and get out before capture. The bribed policemen would sound off a warning by blasting their rifles into the air, and the bribers would know they had to run from Mai Mujuru's abundance. The bribed police would only appear if their superiors were coming to inspect them, or after the hour of foraging was up.

"An hour should be plenty time to make love to Mai Mujuru!" Chris said, sizzling with laughter. Daniel was grinning.

"Yes. Those who get rich from Marange, it seems, get rich doing this. Those who will remain poor will stay in Mufakose and Mbare."

It was tough but they knew it was the truth. They had very little chance, but they had come, so they had to try. They had to dance around the police.

"I still don't know how we are going to see the diamonds in this dark night. Are we going to use candles, or maybe torches? Or maybe we could use our cell phones."

Chris gave Daniel another empty 5 kg pack before answering him;

"No, we don't use torches. The police would see us straight away and we would be dead meat. What we'll do is dig some soil and pack it in this plastic, and then tomorrow morning we will wash it with water and find whatever is there."

The first day, they entered the area at around 8 at night. Before they started digging, they heard the *cluck cluck* sounds of the AK47 as the killing orgy started, so they ran into the nearby mountains with the little soil they had dug and waited for the police to leave the area. An hour later, they returned to the fields. The police came back, and Chris and Daniel ran off. They returned a little bit later and continued digging for the *ngodas*. That first day they did all that with no success. The second day, they tried again and got nothing. But they didn't tire. The third day they tried again, got their 5kgs packets filled up with soil, washed it on the morning of the fourth day, and Chris found his first *ngoda*. He sold it for Z$600 billion dollars, and bought food. Only bread and milk! But it was a welcome relief. They had their first real meal in over three days. Galvanised by the food, that fourth day they went into the fields again- and nothing. They became more and more desperate. So, on the fifth day, that's when they tried invading the fields during day light and met with tragedy.

Now Chris was alone. It was only a few days ago when they'd been so geared up to earn a living through this illegal mining endeavour. Now he had to confront the evidence of their failure. Meat flies were now gorging themselves on Daniel's hot blood, dripping as if from everywhere. He stood there transfixed for some minutes. He couldn't even bow down and howl in grief.

He knew he couldn't raise Daniel from the dead. He had to continue living for the sake of Daniel, who had sacrificed his life to save him. So, he took his friend's shoes, his watch and cell phone. He took the packets of soil and left Daniel there. He knew the bastards who had killed Daniel would come back later with their vehicles and cart his remains off the fields for burial in the same graveyard where his family members who had died from cholera were buried. He would not visit Daniel in his final resting place. He wouldn't even be able to identify him, for they never put inscriptions on those graves. The following morning he washed the two packs with water and found nothing.

The bread and milk were done with. He couldn't think of spending more days eating wild fruits. Rather, he sold Daniel's worn out shoes, Daniel's spare shirt, their cell phones and Daniel's watch.

At Beitbridge, he bribed some border gangsters to help him cross into South Africa illegally. He was stripped of any loose change and abandoned just after crossing Limpopo. He had to find his way through on foot to Musina refugee camp. He processed a refugee permit worth only six months and became one of the refugees.

Chris hasn't been to his rural home for years, almost 6 years now. Marange doesn't remind him of his childhood anymore, but of the foraging, fondling, caressing of Mai Mujuru's breast and the death of his friend Daniel. He has never returned home to see those of his family left behind after the Cholera scourge. He has never seen his beautiful Concillia, whom God stole from him through the Johanne Marange Sect. He knows that she died during a difficult pregnancy. He hasn't seen his parents for years either. He later heard that the Mujurus were still there, hidden under other names. Nowadays, there is only one name being heard in Marange:

Mbada Diamond Mining Company. Maybe the beast Mbada had suckled all the milk in Mai Mujuru's breast.

Chapter 18: A HERO OF ZEROES

Without realising what he was getting himself involved into, this man took a doll thing with him to Zimbabwe, and did an appeasement ceremony. It came alive as a Tokoloshi, grew a bit to about the knee's level. He named it "Matipedza". Matipedza (literary meaning, you-have-finished-killing-us) called this man "Father", and told Father to feed him with blood, any blood would do fine. Father went to his cattle kraal and killed a cow and gave Matipedza the blood, which he drunk. When Matipedza was satisfied he started throwing up money, not blood. He puked lots and lots of dollars, all over the spare bedroom where father had done this ceremony, and where he was keeping Matipedza hidden from his wife and family. He had told everyone not to visit the room. He would also take the keys to this room with him, everywhere he would go; afraid someone might try to access this room. Father didn't waste time in counting the money. He simply collected it and locked it in a big black trunk he kept in that room.

When growing up, well when Joseph started his first grade class, he used to struggle to count from 1 up to 10, and by the time he reached about grade 7, he knew how to count up to 1 000 000. And, 1 000 000 seemed to be such a colossal number, and beyond that, it was a world of speculation. All the countries had populations that counted in millions, then. And then, 1 000 000 000 came about in his secondary school years, in the form of those Western Multinational Corporations, which had net-worth in excess of billions of dollars. 1 000 000 000 000 came about with the

US budget, in the late nineties. All these billions and trillions of things were not appearing in his world of things.

In his world of things though there were the stories that dealt with figures, monetary figures and there is this particular one that he remembered. The man was a hard worker, and for years he had failed to break through in life. He had given up hope of succeeding in the country. He had stopped trying to change his situation. He left for South Africa with the intention of trying to get a better job or better prospects there. He had to walk for three months to reach South Africa, like how the people were doing then. It was in the late fifties- early sixties- the days of the so-called Wenera Era in South Africa, when the gold mining explosion attracted the hoards of people from other African countries. So, when this man arrived in South Africa he tried to get a job, but failed. He failed to break through, again, and it was in a foreign land! He became desperate.

He consulted a Sangoma (a traditional faith-healer) and asked this Sangoma why things were not always working with him. He was told he was forsaken, cursed in life, was never meant to succeed in anything, and that he had to get help from other worlds to succeed. Upon which he was given this doll of a thing, which he was told was going to help him in accruing wealth. He was told he had to feed this thing, whatever it wants. But, first of all, that he had to take it with him to Zimbabwe, and do some appeasement ceremony to activate it into life so that it would start helping him accruing wealth.

There was also a time, by the end of 2004, when Joseph's payslip reached the 1 000 000-00 mark. He had to withdraw, from the bank, lots and lots of bills to get by, to procure some basic necessities. It reminded him of this story of the Tokoloshi that puked money. Joseph could throw the money, from his salary, in his bedroom, and it would cover every surface in his bedroom, like the money that Matipedza would throw up in that spare bedroom. But, like some elfin child of some sort, the Reserve Bank Governor of the country, decided to make Joseph feel poor again, by slashing three zeroes from the currency, and from his payslip, as well. All of a sudden, instead of getting 30 000 000-00, he only got 30 000-00, in August 2006. 30 000-00 couldn't cover every surface in his room, no. But, he never had an intention of getting a Tokoloshi to deal with this insult. He knew how dangerous those things were. He knew of the story of Matipedza.

Matipedza demanded blood, every day, from Father and, Father killed the cows. At first he kept as much of the meat as he could, but when the carcasses mounted he didn't know where to put all that meat. He lied to his family that some cow hustler was killing his livestock. The only problem was he hadn't had any foresight to the situation. He hadn't created a butcher shop, such that; he got overwhelmed by the situation. It also meant that he had to procure some more beasts of cows to satiate the thirst of Matipedza. That created catastrophic problems. Some day and, when he had failed to procure some cow to behead, this Tokoloshi killed his first son and drunk the blood. Afterwards, he puked lots and lots of money. There was nothing Father could do about that.

There was also nothing Joseph could do about his zeroes, as well. He would console himself, that someday, if he were to become the governor of the Reserve Bank, he would have to correct this anomaly by claiming back his three zeroes. Father couldn't claim back his son from the dead. That elfin child, the

Reserve Bank Governor, like the Tokoloshi, started twitching inflation figures. He would say it was 20 000%, when it actually was 200 000 %. And Matipedza, when he had tasted human's blood started demanding for more human blood, every day. He killed the children of this man, one after another. Father didn't know what to do with this Matipedza. He couldn't buy back his kids with the money Matipedza was puking. So, he decided to visit another Sangoma, now a Zimbabwean Sangoma.

He was told he had to take another Tokoloshi, which would eat Matipedza. He would take both these Tokoloshis across the river and dump them there. The Sangoma told him they would kill each other, and that, after all, no Tokoloshi can be able to cross the river. This Sangoma knew they would, but he lied to Father for other reasons. This Sangoma had his own Tokoloshis he didn't know what to do with, so he figured it was an opportunity to do away with these. Father asked for three of these, so that they would be able to accomplish the job of killing Matipedza without fail. Father accepted three more Tokoloshis, which he took with him back home. The morrow morning he took these four Tokoloshis across the river, did some appeasement ceremony he had been told to do by the Sangoma, dumped these four Tokoloshis and crossed the river back, and left the four monsters to kill each other across the river. He returned home. When he arrived home he found the four Tokoloshis there- waiting for him at the door. Matipedza was so angry with father. He slapped Father so hard, bellowing in a huge voice, accusing Father of abandoning them.

"Father, why did you leave us across the river? Did you want to abandon us? Don't ever do that to us again, Father. Do you hear me?" Matipedza warned Father as he slapped him harder. Father had never been slapped like that, all his life. He fell down on his knees and started begging Matipedza not to beat him again, shouting at the highest of his voices.

"I won't do that again, son... I am so sorry, son.... Please don't beat me again, please, please..."

"I forgive you, Father." Matipedza said and giggled sniggerly, and the other three Tokoloshis joined in, giggling in amusement and mirth.

"I want food, Father; I want blood, and I want Mother's blood, Father." Matipedza demanded.

"I can buy you a cow tomorrow, son. Won't you sleep without eating today, Matipedza my son, please?"

"No, Father. I am so hungry. We had to walk all the way from the river. I need your wife's blood, Father. Mother's blood will satisfy the hunger." Matipedza said that as he licked his lips, smacking them salivating, moistening his dry mouth.

"Please don't ask for that, son." Father tried to plead with Matipedza.

"That's what I want Father, or else we will..."

"Ok, Matipedza, you can have my wife."

So, those Tokoloshis killed the wife of Father and drunk her blood throughout that night. Father didn't sleep that night, afraid of those Tokoloshis, that; they might come for him. He didn't know what to do with these monsters, as well. In the morning he put those Tokoloshis in the bag and told them he was going to his native rural home where the rest of his relatives were, so that he could provide blood to them. When he arrived at the bus stop and when he was boarding the bus, he left the bag with those Tokoloshis outside. He was trying to abandon them, again. When the bus was leaving with Father, those Tokoloshis got out of the bag and saw the bus leaving, with their father. They started chasing the bus, calling the driver to wait for them. But, nobody could hear them. Father was happy he had done away with those Tokoloshis. But, they chased it for nearly five kilometres to the next bus stop. When the driver stopped the bus to collect some more fares, those Tokoloshis caught up with the bus and, secretly- as invisible beings- entered the bus. They came to where Father was sited, and took a heavy breath, and Matipedza whispered in the ears of Father.

"*Topotcha tachara bapa* (we were almost left behind, father)."

Father was surprised to hear Matipedza's voice speaking besides him. He knew he was in hot soup so he apologised quietly to Matipedza, begging him not to beat him, saying that he had forgotten to bring the bag inside when boarding the bus. Matipedza said.

"Don't worry, Father. We are now together, and that's all that matters. At least we are going to have a lot of food where we are going, Father."

Father whispered, "Yes, you are going to have all the food you want, son."

Those monsters giggled quietly to themselves.

As the Reserve Bank governor giggled with mirth at Joseph, and as he would pile up insults on him, in his speeches, in his Operation Sunrise programmes, his monetary talks- how much Joseph had pinned with revenge when those insults were being imposed on him, wily-nilly!

Every month, he would watch the zeroes returning back on his payslip. He couldn't help gushing with silent mirth when he hit back on 1000 000-00, again. It was a comfort knowing that there was someone out there who was working flat out to beat the elfin child, at his game of zeroes, as well; but Joseph still pined for his three zeroes, just like a one-legged person would miss and pine for his other leg. He felt they were an inseparable part of his life. This coming back of the zeroes on his payslip reminded him of how Father was failing to dump those Tokoloshis for good. How Matipedza and his crew would find their way back to Father, after every attempt by Father to do away with them. Now, Father was on a journey, a wrong journey. In actual fact, Father was on his way out of the country. He was on his way to Zambia, though he had lied to the monsters that he was on his way to his rural home. Even though he had tried to abandon them at the bus stop, they were now with him again, in the bus to Zambia.

The zeroes kept accumulating, yet the Reserve Bank governor continued twitching inflation figures. When the governor felt he couldn't keep up with the inflation figures anymore he stopped pegging it, in July 2008, at 231 000 000 %. Like the elfin child that he was and, all of a sudden, he swiped off ten zeroes from the highest currency denominator. 100 000 000 000-00 dollars became 10 dollars. How so spitefully he was! So that, he was beating Joseph on two fronts, and it eventually became so apparent to Joseph that he would never be the Reserve Bank Governor, he decided to revenge back through this story. Whilst he was thinking of it, he didn't know what punishment he would meet out on that trouble-some child. But, like an inspiration, he would return each and every zero the governor has tempered with on the currency! This gets suggested in his mind and he bends to it like the jack pines in the wind. He would search around for an independent institute that would measure the inflation figures for him.

For his 50 000 000-00 note, he is adding back the 13 zeroes so that this is what it would read like, Z$ 500 000 000 000 000 000 000-00. That means the highest note is 500 sextillion dollars. In his wildest dreams, he never thought he would have this kind of revenge! It felt so beautiful beating the governor at his game of zeroes. Some institution, CATO Institute, thinking along those designs of his, measured the inflation figures. Here are the zeroes, no, no, no, not 231 000 000 %, after all this is not July, but December 2008.

How about 98 700 sextillion percent for the inflation! No. no. no, not in words, and here are the zeroes, 98 700 000 000 000 000 000 000%. Mind boggling stats! Eventually he felt he had his revenge in full. He is sorry, he would seem like he was crowing but this was the only revenge he could think of, since he would never, in his entire life, be the Reserve Bank Governor, or even hire a Tokoloshi to accrue wealth for himself.

Matipedza had had enough of Father's lying, as well. So, he confronted Father when he realised the journey home was becoming a journey out of the country, as they approached Chirundu Border Post. He and the other Tokoloshis became visible to the people in this bus journey, and Matipedza asked Father, in a high voice, so that everyone else in that bus heard him clearly.

"Father, I am now hungry, you have also been lying to us that we are going home when, in actual fact, you are taking us far away from our food." And the other Tokoloshi said,

"Please Father, tell us who in this bus we could eat, we are so hungry. We haven't eaten for the whole of the day, and it's now night's fall." And yet another said,

"We are so hungry, Father"

Father tried to talk silently to Matipedza, but the people in this bus journey heard him clearly.

"Please son, don't ask that from me. We will find food where we are going, please be patient with me, son."

People in the bus knew what was happening, so they asked the driver to stop the bus. Then, they asked Father to leave the bus with his Tokoloshis. But the Tokoloshis refused to leave the bus. They knew if they leave the bus they will be defrauded of their food. They started strangling and gorging a young girl nearby; guzzling her blood in the sight of everyone. The people tried to beat those monsters, off the girl, but were slapped hard by those monsters. People in this bus, including the father of this girl, left the bus in a stampede, afraid they would be the next to be eaten, leaving that girl behind, being gorged at by those monsters.

When they were out of the bus someone asked the people to help him, in pushing Father back in the bus, who had also run out of the bus, so that he could face the consequences of his deeds; also thinking that if Matipedza and his crew got some more blood, they wouldn't alight out of the bus to kill them. The people helped in pushing Father back into the bus, and they locked him inside with his Tokoloshis. Then, another person said they should burn the bus with these monsters inside so that they would kill them. Before he had finished his statement, a matchstick was already out, being proffered by another man. Even though the driver and conductor of this bus tried to dissuade these people from burning the bus, they couldn't stop them. The people lighted the bus on fire. They moved to a safe distance as they enjoyed listening to, and hearing Father and his Tokoloshis crying; bellowing in painful voices, as they got roasted in the fire.

End

Ps: But, before Joseph had finished thinking of this revenge story, and whilst he was still wallowing in his revenge, that elfin child struck again, and all of a sudden, he removed 12 zeroes from the currency!

Chapter 19: NYAKASIKANA

He has been working in this mine for a couple of years now. Percival was born in this area with the mine. He had grown up here, did his schooling at Marange primary and secondary schools, failed his "O" levels and for years he didn't have a job, a career, or anything to fall on, or anywhere to go. He had survived by doing odd jobs around the Chiadzwa Villages, and then a miracle happened, five years before.

She was his sister, Agnes was. One night she woke up the whole household. She was roaring in a high voice in the girl's hut, possessed by a spirit. Their mother, father and everyone rushed to the girl's quarters to see what had possessed the usually quiet girl to create such hullabaloo in the middle of the night. Percival was hard on the heels of his parents to his sister's hut. Agnes was the middle child, and often quiet and well behaved, so it even surprised and troubled Percival, why? When they entered the girl's hut, Agnes was thrashing around, roaring, booing; now talking in a huge voice, a male's voice. The voice had inflections of an unusual homage, to something mysterious and elemental, like the wind, the eye of a tornado would speak if it speaks at all. It sends shivers down Percival's spine. Everyone knew what was happening to Agnes, for something spiritual had taken hold of her

"I am the unknown. You should know me as the Spirit of the Unknown. I gave birth to this land. I was here in the beginning. I have seen my people suffering over the billion-fold years…"

"Talk Sekuru, the Spirit of the Unknown. We are listening; your grandchildren are listening…" They chorused as they clapped their

156

hands. Sekuru shook as if a sheep is shaking off water, off its body, sizzling inside his being.

"I want my Nhekwe yeBute, Vazukuru." Sekuru admonished his grandchildren.

"Yes, Sekuru." Agnes's mother runs off to her bedroom. Nhekwe yeBute is grounded and roasted tobacco (Snuff Bute) in its container. The container is made usually of a holed, on one side, water reed or chunk of wood. So this tobacco is stored inside this hole, which is usually cased by a small stick. She brought back Nhekwe yeBute with the roasted and grounded tobacco she had been sniffing herself. She gave this to Sekuru. After Sekuru had taken a huge sniff of Snuff Bute, a couple of times, he sneezed, groaned, and nodded his head, appeased with the tobacco, and continued.

"I have seen how much you have suffered over the years, grandchildren. It has been because of Nyakasikana, the virgin girl. She died in mysterious circumstances, was murdered by a suitor who had failed to win her hand. Nyakasikana wasn't made for any man, but for the gods. That's why the gods have punished you, people. How can a mortal being, like man, could marry Nyakasikana, could even kill her, the wife of the gods! Her spirit has made life hard for Marange. She is the one who has dammed all the waters in the clouds, such that this place hasn't had adequate rains in generations and generations. Nyakasikana tells me she now wants to rest. She has agreed to rest now. I will show you where her bones lays unburied. On top of which you will find *Hata yaNyakasikana*, a python snake rolled into a circle. What the people of this area have to do is to brew beer, kill a fat bull and celebrate, giving offerings of *Kahari keMutsunga* (a small clay pot of the best beer) to Nyakasikana. This *Kahari keMutsunga* will be taken by me in this embodiment, the King, the Chief and the royal family, including you, my family. I will direct you to the place where you have to put that small pot of Mutsunga Beer, inside this ringed snake. You have to wait for a week to let Nyakasikana and the gods quench their thirst, and then return back to the place. Now, do what I have told you to do, children. I will tell you what next to do after you have carried forward all that I have told you to do now."

They thanked the Spirit of the Unknown and took her word to the Chief. The Chief took the word to the King, and the two came to see Sekuru and were told the same things. So the Chief, the King and the entire Chiadzwa Community did as they had been told to do by Sekuru. They brewed beer and on the appeasement day, they took *Kahari keMutsunga* to the place, being guided by the Spirit of the Unknown. It is a place they have always passed through without any problems over the years. It was just off the banks of Chiadzwa River, in the valley between the mountains. Sekuru lead them to this place possessed of the Spirit of the Unknown, and as per the promise they found *Hata yaNyakasikana*, a circled python snake, and placed that *Kahari keMutsunga* into the circle it had created, gave thanks and praised Sekuru, Nyakasikana, and the gods and medium spirits of this place. Then they left for home, leaving Sekuru behind. Sekuru also told them they had to return back, in a week's time, and exhume the bones of Nyakasikana where they had left *Hata yaNyakasikana* and the *Kahari keMutsunga* beer. Sekuru said he would find his way home one day, and that they didn't have to cry for him if they wanted his spirit to rest in peace, and not to come back to trouble them in the future. They returned back home. They didn't shed a tear. After a week they returned back to the place to find the place bare of *Hata yaNyakasikana, Kahari keMutsunga*, and Sekuru the Spirit of the Unknown. They knew Sekuru had found his way home in the nearby pool, that Sekuru was the spirit of the mermaid now. So the Chief, the King and their subjects dug into the soil to exhume the bones of Nyakasikana, as they had been told to do by Sekuru, so that they could burry Nyakasikana properly.

They had dug a few feet when they hit on a colourful bunch of stones, beautiful glassy stones, and they knew what they were. Nyakasikana had given them a livelihood. The Spirit of the Unknown, the gods, Nyakasikana and the medium spirits had quenched their thirst, from the pot of Mutsunga Beer and, were now pleased with the Marange people. They were so happy.

Chapter 20: HELL'S HEVEAN-SENT REFUGEES

When he arrived at the gates of heaven he found St Simon Peter at the gates. He was told heaven was not his resting place, so he had to go to hell. His bags were so heavy and full of all the thousands of people he had killed in his lifetime, and so he failed to carry the bags with him to hell. He left them with Simon Peter by heaven's gate. When he arrived at hell he asked Satan to send Hunzwi, Gezi and other little devils to go and pick up his bags at heaven's gates, of which Satan did that. He also sent Hitler, Mussolini, and Pol Pot with those little devils. When those devils arrived at heaven's gates, Simon had taken the bags inside heaven and closed heaven's gates.

So those little devils started climbing the walls of heaven, in order to retrieve the bags. When St Peter saw them he couldn't help remarking to St John whom he was talking to;

"Surely Uncle Bob is so bad, for he has barely been in hell and already there are refugees coming from hell that you can see are trying to scale heaven's walls, and to enter heaven illegally."

Chapter 21: Raising A Cain Again

They were brothers from the same womb, Cain and Abel. Cain brought to the Lord produce from his fields, which was not good enough in the eyes of the Lord. Abel brought fat portions from some of the firstborns of his flock, which pleased the Lord.

Cain killed Abel.

I know I am not saying anything new here. You have already heard of this story,

77 times!

And then the Lord asked Cain, "Where is your brother, Abel."

And he replied,

"I don't know, am I my brother's killer?"

Chapter 22: Leonard

He was twenty three years old, when he finished his 'O' levels, five years before. With so much hope of getting a good job, he had moved to the city of Harare, *H-Town*. That's where most young hopeful man would move to after school, in search of brighter prospects. In the first days in this city he could spend the whole odd day, patrolling, more like a soldier the industrial streets, hunting for a job. He had done all that he could, and here and there, behind closed doors, people with relatives, people who could bribe the foreman were taken in. He didn't have money to pay for a taxi into the industrial area from his high density township suburb of Glen Norah, he had walked everyday to the industrial areas, then let alone money to bribe the marketplace-souled foreman.

They wanted to have more and more. If you give them money in exchange with employment, it won't end there. At your first payday they would be expecting more, and at your next paydays some more and more. It would continue like that. It was the suk-mentality- it was the mosquito's suk-mentality, and it had sunk deep roots into the whole fibre of the society. Leonard knew he had to either dance to its tune or face a cold stomach every night, but he couldn't bring himself to do that yet. He had told himself that one day things would look up for him.

But for five years he had walked every road surface of the industrial areas, the city centre, the residential areas and nothing good came out of it. Thus a few days before Christmas of his twenty third year, he bed his widowed aunt farewell. He couldn't keep burdening her anymore, draining the little she earned from selling fruits, vegetables and other small wares on the streets. She had two school going children to look after, as well. It was chaotic to raise money for these children's school fees, let alone for their daily upkeep.

Leonard had returned back home, to his struggling, live by the hands, toil all day long parents who were still farming a spent up plot of six acres and a garden patch by the river. He was shattered. He felt betrayed by the kind of life he had met up with in the bright diamond lighted city of Harare. Only home, in the far backward black water rural setting could help sooth his benumbed feelings and cold hopes. He had helped his family doing the weeding and many other field jobs at their family. When the crops had come toward harvesting, that's when everything, his life, his hopes and feelings had taken another dangerous spiralling turn.

Leonard was coming from the local shops, Chirowamhangu shopping centre, going home in Sharamba village, tucked in the banks of the Nyajezi River, where he stayed. He had been send, by his mother, to procure their thin grocery of kapenta fish, 750ml bottle of cooking oil, 500 grams of salt at Chirowamhangu shops. He had met Mr. Karidza, who stayed at Hogo village, to the north of Sharamba village, a couple of villages from Sharamba. He had heard a lot about Mr. Karidza and his associations with the newly formed political party, Democratic Alliance Labour Party. Mr Karidza was its chairman for the Nyanga constituency. It turned out Karidza, a friend of their neighbour Mr. Maboreke, was going to his friend's place, to discuss with Mr. Maboreke his possibility of taking over the chairmanship of the Sedze cell, after the incumbent of that seat had been killed in political motivated violence. Karidza was an affable frank man in his late fifties. He had no children of his own, so any young person was always special to him.

He knew how to befriend young people who would pass for his kids, if he had any. He found in these young people the kids he never got; they had failed to conceive in their marriage. These two, Leonard and Karidza had talked about life in the city of Harare, life in the whole country, life in their area, the failures and progress of the whole country, how and when things had gone wrong, and their hopes now. This had become the first time since his returning from Harare that Leonard had been able to talk to anyone, how he felt and had fared in Harare. What hopes he still had for himself? There was this way in which Karidza seemed to unlock Leonard's inner self and make him pour his heart out, his fears, his frustrations and his hopes. Somehow he didn't find it unthinkable when Karidza offered him the constituent's leadership of the youth league of DALP. It simply was the correct thing to do.

This had given birth to the satisfaction he now felt as he walked along the road to Nyatate service centre. He had used the central road to Nyatate because it was the nearest way to reach Nyatate. He had a meeting to catch up with in Dandadzi village, just a stone's throw from Nyatate Service Centre. This road was also safe because it snaked through people homes. There was little possibility of getting abducted by the thugs of the other party, Jongwe party, who were terrifying, beating and kidnapping people into submitting to this party, especially in the Sanyabako and Tenga villages, where the other road to Nyatate would go through.

Their meeting came to an early end that day, due to five youths from Tenga village who were making unnecessary disturbances and interjections, throwing rowdy statements and threatening everyone there, promising everyone at the meeting a beating if they continued attending it. These youths, Thomas, Arnold, Christopher, Taurai and Paul had been to school with Leonard, at the adjacent Nyatate Secondary School, 5 years before, but they were not quiet friends with Leonard, even during school years. These were from Jongwe party and were the ones who had been abducting, killing and beating up people in their constituency. These disturbances had forced the Nyatate branch chair, Mr Guta, to call for the disbanding of the meeting before its actual stretch.

Something wasn't right, somehow. Leonard felt it in his bones, as he trudged in the autumn dusk back home. There was something in his bones that screamed something he didn't seem to hear, telling him to seek shelter in the homes he was passing through in the Magaya village, the last village before his Sharamba village. He disdained it. He was almost home. He told himself he was just scared because it was night and he was entering a stretch of forest that had no homes. It was far away from Nyatate so he told himself he had no fear of those youths from Jongwe party, who had stayed behind in their village, Tenga village, which was next to Dandadzi village, to the other side of Nyatate centre.

As he crossed Nyajezi River he saw some fun shadow ahead of him, so he stopped and tried to look hard in the darkening night, but couldn't make what it was. Then, he heard the whooshing sound of something flying towards him. He thought it was a bird so he ducked a bit, thinking it would miss him, but before he finished ducking he was hit, blinded by that duck, on the forehead. It was a stone and, he collapsed on the bridge and fainted.

They beat him with all sorts of traditional weaponry, rods, sticks, axes, pangas, cutting into his flesh. They cut him into pieces and defecated on his pieces and left him dead. Leonard was discovered by the first bus driver that used that road, which plied Nyatate to Harare route, cut into pieces, by the side of the road, off the bridge.

Chapter 23: TREE OF THE YEAR.

Percival remembers someday, always with grief, pain, and regret. Percival and his friend, Jemmies were digging. And, without preamble, the police helicopters and dogs were upon them. They started running towards the mountains. On that day, Jemmies had just dug out of the soil this huge glass diamond. They had promised each other they would share on the wealth. When the police started chasing them and were catching up with them, Jemmies couldn't abide the thought of losing that glass diamond to these police thugs. So, in the eyes of the police, he swallowed it and waited to be captured. But that day the police were in a foul mood. In other instances, they could have taken him to their jails, and forced him to drink stomach cleaning substances and recover their diamonds. But in this instance, they took Jemmies by the shoulders, and in Percival's sights, Jemmies was sliced by the middle. They searched for their diamond which they found in his guts. Percival couldn't run. He was spell bound as he watched his friend being gutted by the stomach, like as if they were opening a plastic bag and got their glass diamond. After recovering their diamond, they also wanted to cut Percival into pieces, but he found his voice, as he begged them not to do that, since he hadn't swallowed any diamonds. For some time they debated among themselves. Lucky was on his side that day, so he wasn't killed. They eventually took him with them, and he was jailed without trial, in Mutare prisons, for illegally mining in his home area.

Now, it is five years when everything had happened. In those five years a lot of things had happened, as well. He has never seen his sister, Agnes. He has never seen his friend, Jemmies. He knows he will never see them, again. Percival has come to accept that it had happened, and that it's something he had to carry with him for the rest of his life.

There were those months on end when the whole of Chiadzwa had woken up to the realisation that their place was a very rich place. There were those days the villagers had dug all over the place trying to find the coveted diamonds, the bones of Nyakasikana, so that they would rest her bones. Percival had also dug the place and found the *ngodas*, the industrial diamonds. The entire country had smelt of this and descended on Chiadzwa, to find the bones of Nyakasikana, to quench the hunger in their bellies. The authorities descended too; to control things, and chased everyone out of the place. The battles assumed and it became a country at war with its people.

He had to spend a year in the prison cells in Mutare, knowing full well that his friend, Jemmies, was dead. When he eventually got out of the prison he just didn't want to hear of anything to do with the diamonds, so he moved in with a relative in Mutare, and maintained a simple life in the city. He was doing odd jobs in the city's township of Sakubva, where he stayed. After all, he knew he had to heal inside. And also, there was no illegal mining happening at Marange anymore. The government had got control and was now mining through four companies, including IDMC (Ingwe Diamond Mining Company). A year later he went home, and at that time the Chief had got word through to his subjects that he had negotiated for an opening for the local children to be employed at this company. The King couldn't be left out, so the two demanded for bribes, some in access of a head of cattle, for one to be offered a job under this scheme. Percival knew it was an opportunity he couldn't miss, so he gave the Chief their only cow. He became one of the few local people who were employed by this company, as part of the local outreach project to the community of Marange. But, he had paid for this opportunity. What mattered though to him was he had a job. Few of his local people could afford this cow bribe, so they were a few who got the jobs, and not only from this area, but from the whole country. Most of the workers at this company were from outside the country, even though the country owned over 50 percent of this company's worth.

In the first few months he was on the safe side because he did odd jobs outside the factory, but after six months he was promoted to the grading section. He began to have recurring nightmares, even during the day. When he saw those glass diamonds moving on the conveyor belt, he would see blood dripping out of them, instead of the impurities. So he couldn't touch anything, he couldn't grade the impurities, or even the *ngoda* from glass diamond which he was supposed to be doing. For a long time he would just stand transfixed, seeing blood, seeing his friend's blood, Jemmies blood, dripping from the diamonds. At night he would dream about the killing of his friend. He thought the dreams had gone, when he left the prison and was staying in Mutare, but they started coming back, persecuting him every night. He would see Jemmies being cut, being gutted, just to recover a stone- the diamond he had swallowed. When he woke up he would also remember that he had lost his sister, as well, to these diamonds. He would realise the whole country had lost relatives to these diamonds, too. For a month or so he tried to keep working in this department and deal with his problems. Even though his work was poor, they kept him for some time but when nothing changed, they transferred him back to doing menial jobs. He had none to complain to, to tell about the hallucinations; who would listen to him at this company. He reverted to his entry job

In this job he also had to deal with disillusionment, a deep cutting feeling inside his heart as he witnessed the crowning moments of this company's outreach project to the communities of Chiadzwa, which were always piecemeal and frivolous. The most frivolous of which was every year the company would celebrate "World tree planting day" and, it would plant trees, not a lot of trees to cover up the area it would have deforested, through its mining endeavours. It was always such a spectacle, especially the exact day. He knew this year; the politicos would descend on the place. There would be there, planting at least a tree, and it's always one tree that day that would get publicity. What always amazed him was why the tree, that one tree that will be planted by the Governor of the province would automatically win the, "Tree of the Year" Award. He wondered who would have adjudged it to be the best tree planted, or germinating, or even existing that year in the entire country. He wished someone would have the gumption to stand up to this charade and ask the Governor what modelling, or any other competition this tree would have participated in to be thus enthroned with this proud mantle. But, he knew nobody would ask that question. There were a lot other questions nobody ever asked about this company, the mining of diamonds, about Jemmies, and his little sister, Agnes.

He knew there were no answers.

Chapter 24: Karidza

"Who is it?"

"Open the door!"

"Who is it, what do you want?"

"I said open the fucking door, Karidza!"

"It's the middle of the night, can't you see we are already asleep. Why don't you come early in the morning?"

"Hey Karidza, you heard what I said. Open the door or else…, just know that you will regret it." He knew what they meant. He knew he would be burned inside the house if he continues refusing them this.

Who could these people be? What did they want in the middle of the night? Did this have something to do with what's been going on throughout the whole country? He could only do as he had been told to do. He pushed the blankets to his feet, aimlessly rose from the bed, and so did his wife, Mai Karidza. He whispered to her softly that he wanted her to stay inside. She said she is not leaving him alone to face what was outside, that they were going to come inside the house anyway, to check there was no one inside. He tried to plead with her as she put on her night gown, but she now refused to even look at him, afraid he might dissuade her. She avoided his gaze as she accompanied him to the door. She knew she could only frighten him if he were to see the fear deep down her eyes.

They walked slowly to the door, unsure, like two young people who have suddenly aged, wondering why the problems always beset them, even when they thought they had done enough in a way to solving them or just coming to terms with. They were now old people, Mai Karidza was in her late fifties, and Karidza himself was in his middle sixties. The two had failed to conceive a single child in their thirty-plus years of marriage. They had visited every faith healer they could think of and hear of; every Sangoma, everything, but failed. All that, it seemed now, had helped them to get closer to each other. They became closer and closer the more they failed, and now, they existed for each other, and for this dream they had for the country.

They were grassroots activist for DALP (Democratic Alliance Labour Party). They had been in a lot of hair rising situations before, fighting for this party, for their beliefs, for the other people's beliefs... They had survived beatings, injuries, attempted killings as they did their jobs. The logs kept falling in their paths, forcing them to keep jumping, even when they could barely walk. It was two years since they joined this party, in early 2001. Things were now haywire throughout the country.

At the door, Karidza heaved a heavy sigh as he prepared to open the door. He started opening the door slowly, trying to figure out what awaited him, but he was taken by surprise when a heavy boot smashed heavily on his left jaw from that left side, draining the oxygen gaspingly out of his lungs as he thudded to the floors like a bag of maize grains. His head was outside and the rest of his body was still inside piled on top of his wife, as Mai Karidza cried out in alarm and fear for her husband. She was also trying to raise herself from her husband.

The lights blinkered dangerously from an opening sky. It was a clear sky he was seeing even though it was, in actual fact, a dark night. The stars were coming down in a fast, fierce, transcendental traditional beat of the Jiti music hitting on the climax. They were swirling, round around, like the swirl and dazzling acrobat drifts of the monkeys on tree's branches. But, before the stars could touch him, he gave in to the absorbing darkness which ensnared him soothingly.

Then, still deeper into this darkness, he felt the crack in his side body, and jolted back into consciousness as another boot slammed into his side, that hurt like he has never hurt before. He hallowed with pain, complementing his wife, who had been crying at a high voice as she begged them to stop beating her husband. Nobody seemed to hear their cries; nobody came to help them. They knew the next neighbourhood were hearing their cries but they also knew nobody was coming for the people of the next household were of this party. They knew they could only cry…or hope God would get into the minds of these thugs and stay them away from a killing orgy, but they also knew it was a futile hope.

And then he felt another kick slamming into his stomach, as another boot whammed his face as if kicking an inflated ball. The teeth came down from his gums like blooded gemstones as he grabbed his mouth trying to keep them inside his mouth but he knew he couldn't. He needed to release the pain inside his mouth, so he puked the teeth in a ball of blood, teeth, mucus and spit as another boot knocked the air out of his lungs by his chest, devastating him with pain as he fainted again.

He stared drifting from conscious to out of consciousness as they continued beating him. For long minutes he drifted in and out of consciousness as he still felt the cries of his wife, now being beaten as well, as she hallowed with the pain he now knew she was feeling all over her body. As one group continued beating him he knew the other group was beating his wife, as well. He knew there was nothing he could do about it, neither his wife. He came to the realisation that he had reached his endpoint in life. He was dying, but he had no regrets. He had faced the reality of his existence. He had tried all the best to achieve on the things he believed in. He knew the struggle would continue. It wouldn't end with their killings. As he folded for the last time he knew he was happy.

Mmap Fiction Series

If you have enjoyed *Notes From A Modern Chimurenga: Collected Struggle Stories* consider these other fine books in Mmap Fiction Series from *Mwanaka Media and Publishing*:

The Water Cycle by Andrew Nyongesa
A Conversation…, A Contact by Tendai Rinos Mwanaka
A Dark Energy by Tendai Rinos Mwanaka
Keys in the River: New and Collected Stories by Tendai Rinos Mwanaka
How The Twins Grew Up/Makurire Akaita Mapatya by Milutin Djurickovic and Tendai Rinos Mwanaka
White Man Walking by John Eppel
The Big Noise and Other Noises by Christopher Kudyahakudadirwe
Tiny Human Protection Agency by Megan Landman
Ashes by Ken Weene and Umar O. Abdul

Soon to be released

School of Love and Other Stories by Ricardo Felix Rodriguez
Cycle of Life by Ikegwu Michael Chukwudi

https://facebook.com/MwanakaMediaAndPublishing/

Printed in the United States
By Bookmasters